THE CRACK IN SPACE

BOOKS BY PHILIP K. DICK

The Exegesis of Philip K. Dick

NOVELS

The Broken Bubble
Clans of the Alphane Moon
Confessions of a Crap Artist
The Cosmic Puppets
Counter-Clock World
The Crack in Space
Deus Irae (with Roger Zelazny)
The Divine Invasion
Do Androids Dream of Electric Sheep?
Dr. Bloodmoney
Dr. Futurity
Eye in the Sky
Flow My Tears, the Policeman Said
Galactic Pot-Healer
The Game-Players of Titan
Gather Yourselves Together
Lies, Inc.
The Man in the High Castle
The Man Who Japed
Martian Time-Slip
Mary and the Giant
A Maze of Death
Nick and the Glimmung
Now Wait for Last Year
Our Friends from Frolix 8
The Penultimate Truth
A Scanner Darkly
The Simulacra
Solar Lottery
The Three Stigmata of Palmer Eldritch
Time Out of Joint
The Transmigration of Timothy Archer
Ubik
Ubik: The Screenplay
VALIS
Vulcan's Hammer
We Can Build You
The World Jones Made
The Zap Gun

PHILIP K. DICK

THE CRACK IN SPACE

MARINER BOOKS
HOUGHTON MIFFLIN HARCOURT
Boston   New York

First Mariner Books edition 2011

For information about permission to reproduce selections from this book,
write to Permissions, Houghton Mifflin Harcourt Publishing Company,
215 Park Avenue South, New York, New York 10003.

Originally published in the United States by
Ace Books, Inc., New York, in 1966.

www.hmhbooks.com

Library of Congress Cataloging-in-Publication Data
Dick, Philip K.
The crack in space / Philip K. Dick. — 1st Mariner Books ed.
p. cm.
ISBN 978-0-547-57299-4
1. Presidents — Election — Fiction. 2. Life on other planets — Fiction.
3. Race relations — Fiction. 4. Race — Fiction. I. Title.
PS3554.I3C73 2012
813'.54 — dc22   2011015934

Book design by Melissa Lotfy

DOC 10 9 8 7 6 5 4 3 2 1

THE CRACK IN SPACE

1

THE YOUNG COUPLE, black-baked, dark-skinned, probably Mexican or Puerto Rican, stood nervously at Herb Lackmore's counter and the boy, the husband, said in a low voice, 'Sir, we want to be put to sleep. We want to become *bibs*.'

Rising from his desk, Lackmore walked to the counter and although he did not like Cols — there seemed to be more of them every month, coming into his Oakland branch office of the U.S. Department on Special Public Welfare — he said in a pleasant tone of voice designed to reassure the two of them, 'Have you thought it over carefully, folks? It's a big step. You might be out for, say, a few hundred years. Have you shopped for any *professional* advice about this?'

The boy, glancing at his wife, swallowed and murmured. 'No, sir. We just decided between us. Neither of us can get a job and we're about to be evicted from our dorm. We don't even own a wheel, and what can you do without a wheel? You can't go anywhere. You can't even look for work.' He was not a bad-looking boy, Lackmore noticed. Possibly eighteen, he still wore the coat and trousers which were army-separation issue. The girl had long hair; she was quite small, with black, bright eyes and a delicately-formed almost doll-like face. She never ceased watching her husband.

'I'm going to have a baby,' the girl blurted.

'Aw, the heck with both of you,' Lackmore said in disgust, drawing his breath in sharply. 'You both get right out of here.'

Ducking their heads guiltily the boy and his wife turned and started from Lackmore's office, back outside onto the busy downtown early-morning Oakland, California street.

'Go see an abort-consultant!' Lackmore called after them irritably. He resented having to help them, but obviously someone had to; look at the spot they had gotten themselves into. Because no doubt they were living on a government military pension, and if the girl was pregnant the pension would automatically be withdrawn.

Plucking hesitantly at the sleeve of his wrinkled coat the Col boy said, 'Sir, how do we find an abort-consultant?'

The ignorance of the dark-skinned strata, despite the government's ceaseless educational campaigns. No wonder their women were often preg. 'Look in the phone book,' Lackmore said. 'Under *abortionists, therapeutic*. Then the subsection *advisors*. Got it?'

'Yes, sir. Thank you.' The boy nodded rapidly.

'Can you read?'

'Yes. I stayed in school until I was thirteen.' On the boy's face fierce pride showed; his black eyes gleamed.

Lackmore returned to reading his homeopape; he did not have any more time to offer gratis. No wonder they wanted to become bibs. Preserved, unchanged, in a government warehouse, year after year, until — would the labor market ever improve? Lackmore personally doubted it and he had been around a long time; he was ninety-five years old, a *jerry*. In his time he had put to sleep thousands of people, almost all of them, like this couple, young. And — dark.

The door of the office shut. The young couple had gone again as quietly as they had come.

Sighing, Lackmore began to read once more the pape's article on the divorce trial of Lurton D. Sands, Jr, the most sensational event now taking place; as always, he read every word of it avidly.

This day began for Darius Pethel with vidphone calls from irate customers wanting to know why their Jiffi-scutlers hadn't been fixed. Any time now, he told them soothingly, and hoped that Erickson was already at work in the service department of Pethel Jiffi-scuttler Sales & Service.

As soon as he was off the vidphone Pethel searched among the litter on his desk for the day's copy of £7.5. *Business Report;* he of course kept abreast of all the economic developments on the planet. This alone set him above his employees; this, his wealth, and his advanced age.

'What's it say?' his salesman, Stu Hadley, asked, standing in the office doorway, robant magnetic broom in hand, pausing in his activity.

Silently, Pethel read the major headline.

EFFECTS ON THE NATION'S BUSINESS
COMMUNITY OF A NEGRO PRESIDENT

And there, in 3-D, animated, was a pic of James Briskin; the pic came to life, Candidate Briskin smiled in miniature, as Pethel pressed the tab beneath it. The Negro's mustache-obscured lips moved and above his head a balloon appeared, filled with the words he was saying.

My first task will be to find an equitable disposition of the tens of millions of sleeping.

'And dump every last bib back on the labor market,' Pethel murmured, releasing the word tab. 'If this guy gets in, the nation's ruined.' But it was inevitable. Sooner or later, there would be a Negro president; after all, since the Event of 1993 there had been more Cols than Caucs.

Gloomily, he turned to page two for the latest on the Lurton Sands scandal; maybe that would cheer him up, the political news being so bad. The famous org-trans surgeon had become involved in a sensational contested divorce suit with his equally famous wife Myra, the abort-consultant. All sorts of juicy details were beginning to filter out, charges on both sides. Dr Sands, according to the homeopapes, had a mistress; that was why Myra had stomped out, and rightly so. Not like the old days, Pethel thought, recalling his youth in the late decades of the twentieth century. Now it was 2080 and public — and private — morality had worsened.

Why would Dr Sands want a mistress anyhow, Pethel wondered, when there's that Golden Door Moments of Bliss satellite passing overhead every day? They say there're five thousand girls to choose from.

He, himself, had never visited Thisbe Olt's satellite; he did not approve of it, nor did very many *jerries* — it was too radical a solution to the overpopulation problem, and seniors, by letter and telegram, had fought its passage in Congress back in '72. But the bill had gone through anyhow ... probably, he reflected, because most Congressmen had the idea of taking a jet'ab up there themselves. And no doubt regularly did, now.

'If we whites stick together — ' Hadley began.

'Listen,' Pethel said, '*that time has passed*. If Briskin can dispose of the bibs, more power to him; personally, it keeps me awake at night, thinking of all those people, most of them just kids, lying in those gov warehouses year after year. Look at the talent going to waste. It's — bureaucratic! Only a swollen socialist government would have dreamed up a solution like that.' He eyed his salesman harshly. 'If you hadn't gotten this job with me, even you might —'

Hadley interrupted quietly, 'But I'm white.'

Reading on further, Pethel saw that Thisbe Olt's satellite had grossed a billion U.S. dollars in 2079. Wow, he said to himself. That's big business. Before him was a pic of Thisbe; with cadmium-white hair and little high conical breasts she was a superb sight, an aesthetic as well as a sexual treat. The pic showed her serving male guests of her satellite a tequila sour — an added fillip because tequila, being derived from the mescal plant, had long been illegal on Earth proper.

Pethel touched the word tab of Thisbe's pic and at once Thisbe's eyes sparkled, her head turned, her stable, dense breasts vibrated subtly, and in the balloon above her head the proper words formed.

Embarrassing personal urgency, Mr American businessman? Do as many doctors recommend: visit my Golden Door!

It was an ad, Pethel discovered. Not an informative article.

'Excuse me.' A customer had entered the store and Hadley moved in his direction.

Oh lord, Darius Pethel thought as he recognized the customer. Don't we have his 'scuttler fixed *yet?* He rose to his feet, knowing that he would be personally needed to appease the man; this was Dr Lurton Sands, and because of his recent domestic troubles he had become, of late, demanding and hot-tempered.

'Yes, Doctor,' Pethel said, walking toward him. 'What can I do for you today?' As if he didn't know. Trying to fight off Myra as well as keep his mistress, Cally Vale, Dr Sands had enough problems; he really needed the use of his Jiffi-scuttler. Unlike other customers it was not going to be possible to put this man off.

• • •

Plucking by reflex at his great handlebar mustache, presidential candidate Jim Briskin said tentatively, 'We're in a rut, Sal. I ought to fire you. You're trying to make me out the epitome of the Cols and yet you know I've spent twenty years playing up to the white power structure. Frankly, I think we'd have better luck trying to get the white vote, not the dark. I'm used to them; I can appeal to them.'

'You're wrong,' his campaign manager, Salisbury Heim, said. 'Your appeal — listen and understand this, Jim — is to the dark kid and his wife scared to death their only prospect is winding up bibs in some gov warehouse. "Bottled in bond," as they say. In you these people see . . .'

'But I feel guilty.'

'Why?' Sal Heim demanded.

'Because I'm a fake. I can't close the Dept of SPW warehouses; you know that. You got me to promise, and ever since I've been sweating my life away trying to conceive how it could be done. And there isn't any way.' He examined his wristwatch; one quarter-hour remained before he had to give his speech. 'Have you read the speech Phil Danville wrote for me?' He reached into his disorganized, lumpy coat-pouch.

'Danville!' Heim's face convulsed. 'I thought you got rid of him; give me that.' He grabbed the folded sheets and began going over them. 'Danville is a nut. Look.' He waved the first sheet in Jim Briskin's face. 'According to him, you're going to ban traffic from the U.S. to Thisbe's satellite. That's insane! If the Golden Door is closed, the birth rate will jump back up again where it was — what then? How does Danville manage to counter that?'

After a pause Briskin said, 'The Golden Door is immoral.'

Spluttering, Heim said, 'Sure. And animals should wear pants.'

'There's just got to be a better solution than that satellite.'

Heim lapsed into silence as he read further into the speech. 'And he has you advocate this outmoded, thoroughly discredited planet-wetting technique of Bruno Mini.' He tossed the papers into Jim Briskin's lap. 'So what do you wind up with? You back a planetary colonization scheme tried twenty years ago and abandoned; you advocate closing the Golden Door satellite—you'll be popular, Jim, after tonight. But popular with whom, though? Just answer me; who is this aimed at?' He waited.

There was silence.

'You know what I think?' Heim said presently. 'I think this is your elaborate way of giving up. Of saying to hell with the whole thing. It's how you shed responsibility; I saw you start to do the same thing at the convention in that crazy doomsday speech you gave, that morbid curiosity which still has everyone baffled. But fortunately you'd already been nominated. It was too late for the convention to repudiate you.'

Briskin said, 'I expressed my real convictions in that speech.'

'What, that civilization is now doomed because of this overpopulation biz? Some convictions for the first Col President to have.' Heim got to his feet and walked to the window; he stood looking out at downtown Philadelphia, at the jet-copters landing, the runnels of autocars and ramps of footers coming and going, into and out of every high-rise building in sight. 'I once in a while think,' Heim said in a low voice, 'that you feel it's doomed because it's nominated a Negro and may elect him; it's a way of putting yourself down.'

'No,' Briskin said, with calm; his long face remained unruffled.

'I'll tell you what to say in your speech for tonight,' Heim said, his back to Briskin. 'First, you once more describe your relationship with Frank Woodbine, because people go for space explor-

ers; Woodbine is a hero, much more so than you or what's-his-
name. You know; the man you're running against. The SRCD
incumbent.'

'William Schwarz.'

Heim nodded exaggeratedly. 'Yes, you're right. Then after
you gas about Woodbine — and we show a few shots of you and
him standing together on various planets — then you make a
joke about Dr Sands.'

'No,' Briskin said.

'Why not? Is Sands a sacred cow? You can't touch him?'

Jim Briskin said slowly, painstakingly, 'Because Sands is a
great doctor and shouldn't be ridiculed in the media the way he
is right now.'

'He saved your brother's life. By finding him a wet new liver
just in the nick of time. Or he saved your mother just when . . .'

'Sands has preserved hundreds, thousands, of people. Including plenty of Cols. Whether they were able to pay or not.'
Briskin was silent a moment and then he added, 'Also I met his
wife Myra and I didn't like her. Years ago I went to her; I had
made a girl preg and we wanted abort advice.'

'Good!' Heim said violently. 'We can use that. You made a
girl pregnant — that, when Nonovulid is free for the asking; that
shows you're a provident type, Jim.' He tapped his forehead.
'You think ahead.'

'I now have five minutes,' Briskin said woodenly. He gathered up the pages of Phil Danville's speech and returned them
to his inside coat pouch; he still wore a formal dark suit even in
hot weather. That, and a flaming red wig, had been his trade-
mark back in the days when he had telecast as a TV newsclown.

'Give that speech,' Heim said, 'and you're politically dead.
And if you're . . .' He broke off. The door to the room had opened
and his wife Patricia stood there.

'Sorry to bother you,' Pat said. 'But everyone out here can hear you yelling.' Heim caught a glimpse, then, of the big outside room full of teen-age Briskinettes, uniformed young volunteers who had come from all over the country to help elect the Republican Liberal candidate.

'Sorry,' Heim murmured.

Pat entered the room and shut the door after her. 'I think Jim's right, Sal.' Small, gracefully-built — she had once been a dancer — Pat lithely seated herself and lit a cigar. 'The more naive Jim appears, the better.' She blew gray smoke from between her luminous, pale lips. 'He still has a lingering reputation for being cynical. Whereas he should be another Wendell Wilkie.'

'Wilkie lost,' Heim pointed out.

'And Jim may lose,' Pat said; she tossed her head, brushing back her long hair from her eyes. 'But if he does, he can run again and win next time. The important thing is for him to appear sensitive and innocent, a sweet person who takes the world's suffering on his own shoulders because he's made that way. He can't help it; he has to suffer. You see?'

'Amateurs,' Heim said, and groaned.

The TV cameras stood inert, as the seconds passed, but they were ready to begin; the time for the speech lay just ahead as Jim Briskin sat at the small desk which he employed when addressing the people. Before him, near at hand, rested Phil Danville's speech. And he sat meditating as the TV technicians prepared for the recording.

The speech would be beamed to the Republican-Liberal Party's satellite relay station and from it telecast repeatedly until saturation point had been achieved. States Rights Conservative Democrat attempts to jam it would probably fail, because of the enormous signal-strength of the R-L satellite. The message would get through despite Tompkin's Act, which permitted jamming of political material. And, simultaneously, Schwarz's speech would be jammed in return; it was scheduled for release at the same time.

Across from him sat Patricia Heim, lost in a cloud of nervous introspection. And, in the control room, he caught a glimpse of Sal, busy with the TV engineers, making certain that the image recorded would be flattering.

And, off in a corner by himself, sat Phil Danville. No one talked to Danville; the party bigwigs, passing in and out of the studio, astutely ignored his existence.

A technician nodded to Jim. Time to begin his speech.

'It's very popular these days,' Jim Briskin said to the TV camera, 'to make fun of the old dreams and schemes for planetary colonization. How could people have been so nutty? Trying to live in completely inhuman environments . . . on worlds never designed for Homo sapiens. And it's amusing that they tried for decades to alter these hostile environments to meet human needs — and naturally failed.' He spoke slowly, almost drawlingly; he took his time. He had the attention of the nation, and he meant to make thorough use of it. 'So now we're looking for a planet ready-made, another "Venus," or more accurately what Venus specifically never was. What we had *hoped* it would be: lush, moist and verdant and productive, a Garden of Eden just waiting for us to show up.'

Reflectively, Patricia Heim smoked her El Producto alta cigar, never taking her eyes from him.

'Well,' Jim Briskin said, 'we'll never find it. And if we do, it'll be too late. Too small, too late, too far away. If we want another Venus, a planet we can colonize, *we'll have to manufacture it ourselves.* We can laugh ourselves sick at Bruno Mini, but the fact is, he was right.'

In the control room Sal Heim stared at him in gross anguish.

He had done it. Sanctioned Mini's abandoned scheme of recasting the ecology of another world. Madness revisited.

The camera clicked off.

Turning his head, Jim Briskin saw the expression on Sal Heim's face. He had been cut off there in the control room; Sal had given the order.

'You're not going to let me finish?' Jim said.

Sal's voice, amplified, boomed, 'No, goddam it. No!'

Standing up, Pat called back, 'You have to. He's the candidate. If he wants to hang himself, let him.'

Also on his feet, Danville said hoarsely, 'If you cut him off again I'll spill it publicly. I'll leak the entire thing how you're working him like a puppet!' He started at once toward the door of the studio; he was leaving. Evidently he meant what he had said.

Jim Briskin said, 'You better turn it back on, Sal. They're right; you have to let me talk.' He did not feel angry, only impatient. His desire was to continue, nothing else. 'Come on, Sal,' he said quietly. 'I'm waiting.'

The party brass and Sal Heim, in the control room, conferred.

'He'll give in,' Pat said to Jim Briskin. 'I know Sal.' Her face was expressionless; she did not enjoy this, but she intended to endure it.

'Right,' Jim agreed, nodding.

'But will you watch a playback of the speech, Jim?' She said, 'For Sal's sake. Just to be sure you intend what you say.'

'Sure,' he said. He had meant to anyhow.

Sal Heim's voice boomed from the wall speaker. 'Damn your black Col hide, Jim!'

Grinning, Jim Briskin waited, seated at his desk, his arms folded.

The read light of the central camera clicked back on.

2

AFTER THE SPEECH Jim Briskin's press secretary, Dorothy Gill, collared him in the corridor. 'Mr Briskin, you asked me yesterday to find out if Bruno Mini is still alive. He is, after a fashion.' Miss Gill examined her notes. 'He's a buyer for a dried fruit company in Sacramento, California, now. Evidently Mini's entirely given up his planet-wetting career, but your speech just now will probably bring him back to his old grazing ground.'

'Possibly not,' Briskin said. 'Mini may not like the idea of a Col taking up his ideas and propagandizing them. Thanks, Dorothy.'

Coming up beside him, Sal Heim shook his head and said, 'Jim, you just don't have political instinct.'

Shrugging, Jim Briskin said, 'Possibly you're right.' He was in that sort of mood, now he felt passive and depressed. In any case the damage had been done; the speech was on tape and already being relayed to the R-L satellite. His review of it had been cursory at best.

'I heard what Dotty said,' Sal said. 'That Mini character will be showing up here now; we'll have him to contend with, along with all our other problems. Anyhow, how about a drink?'

'Okay,' Jim Briskin agreed. 'Wherever you say. Lead the way.'

'May I join you?' Patricia said, appearing beside her husband.

'Sure,' Sal said. He put his arm around her and hugged her. 'A good big tall one, full of curiously-refreshing tiny little bubbles that last all through the drink. Just what women like.'

As they stepped out onto the sidewalk, Jim Briskin saw a picket — two of them, in fact — carrying signs.

KEEP THE

WHITE HOUSE WHITE

LET'S KEEP AMERICA CLEAN!

The two pickets, both young Caucs, stared at him and he and Sal and Patricia stared at them. No one spoke. Several homeo-pape camera men snapped pics; their flashbulbs lit the static scene starkly for an instant, and then Sal and Patricia, with Jim Briskin following, started on. The two pickets continued to pace back and forth along their little routes.

'The bastards,' Pat said as the three of them seated them-selves at a booth in the cocktail lounge across the street from the TV studio.

Jim Briskin said, 'It's their job. God evidently meant them to do that.' It did not particularly bother him; in one form or an-other it had been a part of his life as long as he could remember.

'But Schwarz agreed to keep race and religion out of the elec-tion,' Pat said,

'Bill Schwarz did,' Jim Briskin said, 'but Verne Engel didn't. And it's Engel who runs CLEAN, not the SRCD Party.'

'I know darn well the SRCD pays the money to keep CLEAN solvent,' Sal murmured. 'Without their support it'd fold in a day.'

'I don't agree with you,' Briskin said. 'I think there'll always be a hate organization like CLEAN, and there'll always be peo-ple to support it.' After all, CLEAN had a point; they did not want to see a Negro President, and wasn't it their right to feel like that? Some people did, some people didn't; that was perfectly natural. And, he thought, why should we pretend that race is not the issue? It is, really. I am a Negro. Verne Engel is factually correct. The real question was: how large a percentage of the electorate supported CLEAN's views? Certainly, CLEAN did not hurt his feelings; he could not be wounded: he had experienced too much already in his years as a newsclown. In my years, he thought to himself acidly, as an American Negro.

A small boy, white, appeared at the booth with a pen and tablet of paper. 'Mr Briskin, can I get your autograph?'

Jim signed and the boy darted off to join his parents at the door of the tavern. The couple, well-dressed, young, and obviously upper stratum, waved at him cheerily. 'We're with you!' the man called.

'Thanks,' Jim said, nodding to them and trying — but not successfully — to sound cheery in return.

'You're in a mood,' Pat commented.

He nodded. Mutely.

'Think of all those people with lily-white skins,' Sal said, 'who're going to vote for a Col. My, my. It's encouraging. Proves not all of us Whites are bad down underneath.'

'Did I ever say you were?' Jim asked.

'No, but you really think that. You don't really trust any of us.'

'Where'd you drag that up from?' Jim demanded, angry now.

'What're you going to do?' Sal said. 'Slash me with your electro-graphic magnetic razor?'

Pat said sharply, 'What are you doing, Sal? Why are you talking to Jim like that?' She peered about nervously. 'Suppose someone overheard.'

'I'm trying to jerk him out of his depression,' Sal said. 'I don't like to see him give in to them. Those CLEAN pickets upset him, but he doesn't recognize it or feel it consciously.' He eyed Jim. 'I've heard you say it many times. "I can't be hurt." Hell, you sure can. You were hurt just now. You want everyone to love you, White and Col both. I don't know how you ever got into politics in the first place. You should have stayed a newsclown, delighting young and old. Especially the *very* young.'

Jim said, 'I want to help the human race.'

'By changing the ecology of the planets? Are you serious?'

'If I'm voted into office I actually intend to appoint Bruno Mini, without even having met him, director of the space program; I'm going to give him the chance they never let him have, even when they —'

'If you get elected,' Pat said, 'you can pardon Dr Sands.'

'Pardon him?' He glanced at her, disconcerted. 'He's not being tried; he's being divorced.'

'You haven't heard the rumes?' Pat said. 'His wife is going to dig up something criminal he's done so she can dispatch him and obtain their total property. No one knows what it is yet but she's hinted —'

'I don't want to hear,' Jim Briskin said.

'You may be right,' Pat said thoughtfully. 'The Sands divorce is turning nasty; it might backfire if you mentioned it, as Sal wants you to. The mistress, Cally Vale, has disappeared, possibly murdered. Maybe you do have an instinct, Jim. Maybe you don't need us after all.'

'I need you,' Jim said, 'but not to embroil me in Dr Sands' marital problems.' He sipped his drink.

Rick Erickson, repairman for Pethel Jiffi-scuttler Sales & Service, lit a cigarette, tipped his stool back by pushing with his bony knees against his work bench. Before him rested the master turret of a defective jiffi-scuttler. The one, in fact, which belonged to Dr Lurton Sands.

There had always been bugs in the 'scuttlers. The first one

put in use had broken down; years ago, that had been, but the 'scuttlers remained basically the same now as then.

Historically, the original defective 'scuttler had belonged to an employee of Terran Development named Henry Ellis. After the fashion of humans Ellis had not reported the defect to his employers . . . or so Rick recalled. It had been before his time but myth persisted, an incredible legend, still current among 'scuttler repairmen, that through the defect in his 'scuttler Ellis had — it was hard to believe — composed the Holy Bible.

The principle underlying the operation of the 'scuttlers was a limited form of time travel. Along the tube of his 'scuttler — it was said — Ellis had found a weak point, a shimmer, at which another continuum completely had been visible. He had stooped down and witnessed a gathering of tiny persons who yammered in speeded-up voices and scampered about in their world just beyond the wall of the tube.

Who were these people? Initially, Ellis had not known, but even so he had engaged in commerce with them; he had accepted sheets — astonishingly thin and tiny — of questions, taken the questions to language-decoding equipment at TD, then, once the foreign script of the tiny people had been translated, taking the questions to one of the corporation's big computers to get them answered. Then back to the Linguistics Department and at last at the end of the day, back up the tube of the Jiffi-scuttler to hand to the tiny people the answers — in their own language — to their questions.

Evidently, if you believed this, Ellis had been a charitable man.

However, Ellis had supposed that this was a non-Terran race dwelling on a miniature planet in some other system entirely. He was wrong. According to the legend, the tiny people were from Earth's own past; the script, of course, had been ancient

Hebrew. Whether this had really happened Rick did not pretend to know, but, in any case, for *some* breach of company rules Ellis had been fired by TD and had long since disappeared. Perhaps he had emigrated; who knew? Who cared? TD's job was to patch the thin spot in the tube and see that the defect did not reoccur in subsequent 'scuttlers.

All at once the intercom at the end of Rick's workbench blared. 'Hey, Erickson.' It was Pethel's voice. 'Dr Sands is up here asking about his 'scuttler. When'll it be ready?'

With the handle of a screwdriver Rick Erickson savagely tapped the master turret of Dr Sands' 'scuttler. I better go upstairs and talk to Sands, he reflected. I mean, this is driving me crazy. It *can't* malfunction the way he claims.

Two steps at a time, Rick Erickson ascended to the main floor. There, at the front door, a man was just leaving; it was Sands — Erickson recognized him from the homeopape pics. He hurried, reached him outside on the sidewalk.

'Listen, doc — how come you say your 'scuttler dumps you off in Portland, Oregon and places like that? It just can't; it isn't built that way!'

They stood facing each other. Dr Sands, well-dressed, lean and slightly balding, with deeply tanned skin and a thin, tapered nose, regarded him complexly, cautious about answering. He looked smart, very smart.

So this is the man they're all writing about, Erickson said to himself. Carries himself better than the rest of us and has a suit made from Martian mole cricket hide. But — he felt irritation. Dr Sands in general had a helpless manner; good-looking, in his mid-forties, he had an easy-going, bewildered geniality about him, as if unable to deal with or comprehend the forces which had overtaken him. Erickson could see that; Dr Sands had a crushed quality, still stunned.

And yet Sands remained a gentleman. In a quiet, reasonable tone he said, 'But that's what it seems to do. I wish I could tell you more, but I'm not mechanically inclined.' He smiled, a thoroughly disarming smile that made Erickson ashamed of his own gruffness.

'Aw, hell,' Erickson said, backtracking. 'It's the fault of TD — they could have ironed the bugs out of the 'scuttlers years ago. Too bad you got a lemon.' You look like a not too bad guy, he reflected.

'"A lemon,"' Dr Sands echoed. 'Yes, that sums it up.' His face twisted; he seemed amused. 'Well, that's my luck. Everything has been running like this for me, lately.'

'Maybe I could get TD to take it back,' Erickson said. 'And swap you another one for it.'

'No.' Dr Sands shook his head vigorously. 'I want that particular one.' His tone had become firm; he meant what he said.

'Why?' Who would want to keep an admitted lemon? It didn't make sense. In fact, the entire business had a wrong ring to it, and Erickson's keen faculties detected this — he had seen many, many customers in his time.

'Because it's mine,' Sands said. 'I picked it out originally.' He started on, then, down the sidewalk.

'Don't give me that,' Erickson said, half to himself.

Pausing, Sands said, 'What?' He moved a step back, his face dark, now. The geniality had departed.

'Sorry. No offense.' Erickson eyed Dr Sands acutely. And did not like what he saw. Beneath the doctor's suavity there lay a coldness, something fixed and hard. This was no ordinary person, and Erickson felt uneasy.

Dr Sands said in a crisp voice, 'Get it fixed and soon.' He turned and strode on down the sidewalk, leaving Erickson standing there.

Jeez, Erickson said to himself, and whistled. My busted back.

I wouldn't want to tangle with *him,* he thought as he walked into the store.

Going downstairs a step at a time, hands thrust deep in his pockets, he thought: Maybe I'll stick it all back together and take a trip through it. He was again thinking of old Henry Ellis, the first man to receive a defective 'scuttler; he was recalling that Ellis had not wanted to give up his particular one, either. And for good reason.

Back in the service department basement once more, Rick seated himself at the work bench, picked up Dr Sands' 'scuttler-turret and began to reassemble it. Presently, he had expertly restored it to its place and had hooked it back into the circuit.

Now, he said to himself as he switched on the power field. Let's see where it gets us. He entered the big gleaming circular hoop which was the entrance of the 'scuttler, found himself — as usual — within a gray, formless tube which stretched in both directions. Framed in the opening behind him lay his work bench. And in front of him —

New York City. An unstable view of an industriously-active street corner which bordered Dr Sands' office. And a wedge, beyond it, of the vast building itself, the high rise skyscraper of plastic — rexeroid compounds from Jupiter — with its infinitude of floors, endless windows . . . and, past that, monojets rising and descending from the ramps, along which the footers scurried in swarms so dense as to seem self-destructive. The largest city in the world, four-fifths of which lay subsurface; what he saw was only a meager fraction, a trace of its visible projections. No one in his lifetime, even a *jerry,* could view it all; the city was simply too extensive.

See? Erickson grumbled to himself. Your 'scuttler's working okay; this isn't Portland, Oregon — it's exactly what it's supposed to be.

Crouching down, Erickson ran an expert hand over the surface of the tube. Seeking—what? He didn't know. But something which would justify the doctor's insistance on retaining this particular 'scuttler.

He took his time. He was not in a hurry. And he intended to find what he was searching for.

3

THE PLANET-WETTING SPEECH which Jim Briskin delivered that night—taped earlier during the day and then beamed from the R-L satellite—was too painful for Salisbury Heim to endure. Therefore, he took an hour off and sought relief as many men did: he boarded a jet'ab and shortly was on his way to the Golden Door Moments of Bliss satellite. Let Jim blab away about Bruno Mini's crackpot engineering program, he said to himself as he rested in the rear seat of the rising 'ab, grateful for this interval of relaxation. Let him cut his own throat. But at least I don't have to be dragged down to defeat along with him; I'm tempted, sometime before election day, to cut myself loose and go over to the SRCD party.

Beyond doubt, Bill Schwarz would take him on. By an intricate route Heim had already sounded the opposition out. Schwarz had, through this careful, indirect linkage, expressed pleasure at the idea of Heim joining forces with him. However, Heim was not really ready to make his move; he had not pursued the topic further.

At least, not until today. This new, painful bombshell. And at a time when the party had troubles enough already.

The fact of the matter was—and he knew this from the latest polls—that Jim Briskin was trailing Schwarz. Despite the fact that he had all the Col vote, and that included non-Negro dark races such as Puerto Ricans on the East Coast and the Mexicans on the West. It was not a shoo-in by any means. And why was Briskin trailing? Because all the Whites would be going to the pols, whereas only about sixty per cent of the Cols would show up on election day. Incredibly, they were apathetic toward Jim. Perhaps they believed — and he had heard this said — that Jim had sold out to the White power structure. That he was not authentically a leader of the Col people as such. And in a sense this was true.

Because Jim Briskin represented Whites and Cols alike.

'We're there, sir,' the 'ab driver, a Col, informed him. The 'ab slowed, came to rest on the breast-shaped vehicle port of the satellite, a dozen yards from the pink nipple which served as a location-signal device. 'You're Jim Briskin's campaign manager?' the driver said, turning to face him. 'Yeah, I recognize you. Listen, Mr Heim; he's not a sell-out, is he? I heard a lot of folk argue that, but he wouldn't do it; I know that.'

'Jim Briskin,' Heim said as he dug for his wallet, 'has sold out nobody. And never will. You can tell your buddies that because it's the truth.' He paid his fare, feeling grumpy. Grumpy as hell.

'But is it true that —'

'He's working with Whites, yes. He's working with me and I'm White. So what? Are the Whites supposed to disappear when Briskin is elected? Is that what you want? Because if it is, you're not going to get it.'

'I see what you mean, I guess,' the driver said, nodding slowly. 'You infer he's for all the people, right? He's got the interest of the White minority at heart just like he has the Col majority. He's going to protect everybody, even including you Whites.'

'That's right,' Salisbury Heim said, as he opened the 'ab door. 'As you put it, "even including you Whites'". He stepped out on the pavement. Yes, even us, he said to himself. Because we merit it.

'Hello there, Mr Heim.' A woman's melodious voice. Heim turned —

'Thisbe,' he said, pleased. 'How are you?'

'I'm glad to see that you haven't stayed below just because your candidate disapproves of us,' Thisbe Olt said. Archly, she raised her green-painted, shining eyebrows. Her narrow, harliquin-like face glinted with countless dots of pure light embedded within her skin; it gave her eerie, nimbus-like countenance the appearance of constantly-renewed beauty. And she had renewed herself, over a number of decades. Willowy, almost frail, she fiddled with a tassel of stone-impregnated fabric draped about her bare arms; she had put on gay clothes in order to come out and greet him and he was gratified. He liked her very much — had for some time now.

Guardedly, Sal Heim said, 'What makes you think Jim Briskin has any bones to pick with the Golden Door, Thisbe? Has he ever actually said anything to that effect?' As far as he knew, Jim's opinions on that topic had not been made public; at least he had *tried* to keep them under wraps.

'We know these things, Sal,' Thisbe said, 'I think you'd better go inside and talk with George Walt about it; they're down on level C, in their office. They have a few things to say to you, Sal. I know bcause they've been discussing it.'

Annoyed, Sal said, 'I didn't come here —' But what was the use? If the owners of the Golden Door satellite wanted to see him, it was undoubtedly advisable for him to come around. 'Okay,' he said, and followed Thisbe in the direction of the elevator.

It always distressed him — despite his efforts to the contrary — to find himself engaged in conversation with George

Walt. They were a mutation of a special sort; he had never seen anything quite like them. Nonetheless, although handicapped, George Walt had risen to great economic power in this society. The Golden Door Moments of Bliss satellite, it was rumored, was only one of their holdings; they were spread extensively over the financial map of the modern world. They were a form of mutated twinning, joined at the base of the skull so that a single cephalic structure served both separate bodies. Evidently the personality *George* inhabited one hemisphere of the brain, made use of one eye: the right, as he recalled. And the personality *Walt* existed on the other side, distinct with its own idiosyncrasies, views and drives — and its own eye from which to view the outside universe.

A uniformed attendant, a sort of cop, stopped Sal, as the elevator doors opened on level C.

'Mr George Walt wanted to see me,' Sal said. 'Or so Miss Olt tells me, at least.'

'This way, Mr Heim,' the uniformed attendant said, touching his cap respectfully and leading Sal down the carpeted, silent hall.

He was let into a large chamber — and there, on a couch, sat George Walt. Both bodies at once rose to their feet, supporting between them the common head. The head, containing the unmingled entities of the brothers, nodded in greeting and the mouth smiled. One eye — the left — regarded him steadily, while the other wandered vaguely off, as if preoccupied.

The two necks joined the head in such a way that the head and face were tilted slightly back. George Walt tended to look slightly over whomever they were talking to, and this added to the unique impression; it made them seem formidable, as if their attention could not really be engaged. The head was normal size, however, as were both bodies. The body to the left — Sal did not recall which of them it was — wore informal clothing, a cotton shirt and slacks, with sandals on the feet. The right hand body, however, was formally dressed in a single-breasted suit, tie and buttoned gray cape. And the hands of the right body were jammed deep into the trouser pockets, a stance which gave to it an aura of authority if not age; it seemed distinctly older than its twin.

'This is George,' the head said, pleasantly. 'How are you, Sal Heim? Good to see you.' The left body extended its hand. Sal walked toward the two of them and gingerly shook hands. The right hand body, Walt, did not want to shake with him; its hands remained in its pockets.

'This is Walt,' the head said, less pleasantly, then. 'We wanted to discuss your candidate with you, Heim. Sit down and have a drink. Here, what can we fix for you?' Together, the two bodies managed to walk to the sideboard, where an elaborate bar could be seen. Walt's hands opened a bottle of Bourbon while George's expertly fixed an old fashioned, mixed sugar and water and bitters together in the bottom of a glass. Together, George Walt made the drink and carried it back to Sal.

'Thanks,' Sal Heim said, accepting the drink.

'This is Walt,' the common head said to him. 'We know that if Jim Briskin is elected he'll instruct his Attorney General to find ways to shut the satellite down. Isn't that a fact?' The two eyes, together now, fixed themselves on him in an intense, astute gaze.

'I don't know where you heard *that*,' Sal said, evasively.

'This is Walt,' the head said. 'There's a leak in your organization; that's where we heard it. You realize what this means. We'll have to throw our support behind Schwarz. And you know how many transmissions we make to Earth in a single day,'

Sal sighed. The Golden Door kept a perpetual stream of junk, honky-tonk stag-type shows, pouring down over a variety of channels, available to and widely watched by almost everyone in the country. The shows—especially the climactic orgy in which Thisbe herself, with her famous display of expanding and contracting muscles working in twenty directions simultaneously and in four colors, appeared—were a come-on for the activity of the satellite. But it would be duck soup to work in an anti-Briskin bias; the satellite's announcers were slick prose.

Downing his drink he rose and started toward the door. 'Go ahead and stick your stag shows on Jim; we'll win the election anyhow and then you can be *sure* he'll shut you. In fact, I personally guarantee it right now.'

The head looked uneasy. 'Dirty p-pool,' it stammered.

Sal shrugged. 'I'm just protecting the interests of my client; you've been making threats toward him. You started it, both of you.'

'This is George,' the head said rapidly. 'Here's what I think we ought to have. Listen to this, Walt. We want Jim Briskin to come up here to the Golden Door and be photographed publicly.' It added, in applause for itself, 'Good idea. Get it, Sal? Briskin arrives here, covered by all the media, and visits one of the girls; it'll be good for his image because it'll show he's a normal guy— and not some creep. So you benefit from this. And, while he's here, Briskin compliments us.' It added, 'A good final touch but optional. For instance, he says the national interest has—'

'He'll never do it,' Sal said. 'He'll lose the election first.'

The head said, plaintively, 'We'll give him any girl he wants; my lord, we have five thousand to choose from!'

'No luck,' Sal Heim said. 'Now if you were to make that offer to me I'd take you up on it in a second. But not Jim. He's—old-fashioned.' That was as good a way to put it as any. 'He's a Puritan. You can call him a remnant of the twentieth century, if you want.'

'Or nineteenth,' the head said, venomously.

'Say anything you want,' Sal said, nodding. 'Jim won't care.

He knows what he believes in; he thinks the satellite is undignified. The way it's all handled up here, boom, boom, boom — mechanically, with no personal touch, no meeting of humans on a human basis. You run an autofac; I don't object and most people don't object, because it saves time. But Jim does, because he's sentimental.'

Two right arms gestured at Sal menacingly as the head said loudly, 'The hell with that! We're as sentimental up here as you can get! We play background music in every room — the girls always learn the customer's first name and they're *required* to call him by that and nothing else! How sentimental can you get, for chrissakes? What do you *want*?' In a higher-pitched voice it roared on, 'A marriage ceremony before and then a divorce procedure afterward, so it constitutes a legal marriage, is that it? Or do you want us to teach the girls to sew mother hubbards and bloomers, and you pay to see their ankles, and that's it? Listen, Sal.' Its voice dropped a tone, became ominous and deadly. 'Listen, Sal Heim,' it repeated. 'We know our business; don't tell us our business and we won't tell you yours. Starting tonight our TV announcers are going to insert a plug for Schwarz in every telecast to Earth, right in the middle of the glorious chef-d'oeuvre you-know-what where the girls . . . well, you know. Yes, I mean *that* part. And we're going to make a campaign out of this, really put it over. We're going to insure Bill Schwarz' reelection.' It added, 'And insure that Col fink's thorough, total defeat.'

Sal said nothing. The great carpeted office was silent.

'No response from you, Sal? You're going to sit idly by?'

'I came up here to visit a girl I like,' Sal said. 'Sparky Rivers, her name is. I'd like to see her now.' He felt weary. 'She's different from all the others . . . at least, all I've tried.' Rubbing his forehead he murmured, 'No, I'm too tired, now. I've changed my mind. I'll just leave.'

'If she's as good as you say,' the head said, 'it won't require any energy from you.' It laughed in appreciation of its wit. 'Send a fray named Sparky Rivers down here,' it instructed, pressing a button on its desk.

Sal Heim nodded dully. There was something to that. And after all, this *was* what he had come here for, this ancient, appreciated remedy.

'You're working too hard,' the head said acutely. 'What's the matter, Sal? *Are you losing?* Obviously, you need our help. Very badly, in fact.'

'Help, schmelp,' Sal said. 'What I need is a six-week rest, and not up here. I ought to take an 'ab to Africa and hunt spiders or whatever the craze is right now.' With all his problems, he had lost touch.

'Those big trench-digging spiders are out, now,' the head informed him. 'Now it's nocturnal moths, again.' Walt's right arm pointed at the wall and Sal saw, behind glass, three enormous iridescent cadavers, displayed under an ultraviolet lamp which brought out all their many colors. 'Caught them myself,' the head said, and then chided itself. 'No, you didn't; I did. You saw them but I popped them into the killing jar.'

Sal Heim sat silently waiting for Sparky Rivers, as the two inhabitants of the head argued with each other as to which of them had brought back the African moths.

The top-notch and expensive — and dark-skinned — private investigator, Tito Cravelli, operating out of N'York, handed the woman seated across from him the findings which his Altac 3-60 computer had derived from the data provided it. It was a good machine.

'Forty hospitals,' Tito said. 'Forty transplant operations within last year. Statistically, it's *unlikely* that the UN Vital Organ Fund Reserve would have had that many organs available in so limited a time, but it is possible. In other words, we've got nothing.'

Mrs Myra Sands smoothed her skirt thoughtfully, then lit a cigarette. 'We'll select at random from among the forty; I want you to follow at least five or six up. How long will it take for you to do that?'

Tito calculated silently. 'Say two days. If I have to go there and see people. Of course, if I can do some of it on the phone — ' He liked to work through the Vidphone Corporation of America's product; it meant he could stick near the Altac 3-60. And, when anything came up, he could feed the data on the spot, get an opinion without delay. He respected the 3-60; it had set him back a great deal, a year ago when he had purchased it. And he did not intend to permit it to lie idle, not if he could help it. But sometimes —

This was a difficult situation. Myra Sands was not the sort who could endure uncertainty; for her things had to be either this or that, either A or not-A — Myra made use of Aristotle's Law of the Excluded Middle like no one else he knew. He admired her. Myra was a handsome, extremely well-educated woman, light-haired, in her middle forties; across from him she sat erect and trim in her yellow Lunar squeak-frog suit, her legs long and without defect. Her sharp chin alone let on — to Tito at least — the grimness, the no-nonsense aspect, of her personality. Myra was a businesswoman first, before anything else; as one of the nation's foremost authorities in the field of therapeutic abortions, she was highly paid and highly honored . . . and she was well aware of this. After all, she had been at it for years. And Tito respected anyone who lived as an independent business person; after all, he, too, was his own boss, beholden to no one, to no subsidizing organization or economic entity. He and Myra had something in common. Although, of course, Myra would have denied it, Myra Sands was a terrible goddam snob; to her, Tito Cravelli was an *employee* whom she had hired to find out — or rather to establish as fact — certain information about her husband.

He could not imagine why Lurton Sands had married her. Surely it had been conflict — psychological, social, sexual, professional — from the start.

However, there was no explaining the chemistry which joined men and women, locked them in embraces of hate and mutual suffering sometimes for ninety years on end. In his line, Tito had seen plenty of it, enough to last him even a *jerry* lifetime.

'Call Lattimore Hospital in San Francisco,' Myra instructed in her crisp, vigilantly authoritative voice. 'In August, Lurton transplanted a spleen for an army major, there; I think his name was Walleck or some such quiddity as that. I recall, at the time . . . Lurton had had, what shall I say? A little too much to drink. It was evening and we were having dinner. Lurton blurted out some darn thing or other. About "paying heavily" for the spleen. You *know*, Tito, that VOFR prices are rigidly set by the UN and they're not high; in fact they're too low . . . that's the cardinal reason the fund runs out of certain vital organs so often. Not from a lack of supply so much as the existence of too darn many takers.'

'Hmm,' Tito said, jotting notes.

'Lurton always said that if the VOFR only were to raise its rates . . .'

'You're positive it was a spleen?' Tito broke in.

'Yes.' Myra nodded curtly, exhaling streamers of gray smoke that swirled toward the lamp behind her, a cloud that drifted in the artificial light of the office. It was dark outside, now; the time was seven-thirty.

'A spleen,' Tito recapitulated. 'In August of this year. At Lattimore General Hospital in San Francisco. An army major named —'

'Now I'm beginning to think it was Wozzeck,' Myra put in. 'Or is that an opera composer?'

'It's an opera,' Tito said. 'By Berg. Seldom performed, now.' He lifted the receiver of the vidphone. 'I'll get hold of the business office at Lattimore; it's only four-thirty out there on the Coast.'

Myra rose to her feet and roamed restlessly about the office, rubbing her gloved hands together in a motion that irritated Tito and made it difficult for him to concentrate on his call.

'Have you had dinner?' he asked her, as he waited on the line.

'No. But I never eat until eight-thirty or nine; it's barbaric to eat any earlier.'

Tito said, 'Can I take you to dinner, Mrs Sands? I know an awfully good little Armenian place in the Village. The food's actually prepared by humans.'

'Humans? As compared to what?'

'Automatic food-processing systems,' Tito murmured. 'Or don't you ever eat in autoprep restaurants?' After all, the Sands were wealthy; possibly they normally enjoyed human-prepared food. 'Personally, I can't stand autopreps. The food's always so predictable. Never burned, never . . .' He broke off; on the vidscreen the miniature features of an employee at Lattimore had formed. 'Miss, this is Life-factors Research Consultants of N'York calling. I'd like to inquire about an operation performed on a Major Wozzeck or Walleck last August, a spleen transplant.'

'Wait,' Myra said suddenly. 'Now I remember; it wasn't a spleen — it was an islands of Langerhans; you know, that part of the pancreas which controls sugar production in the body. I remember because Lurton got to talking about it because he saw me putting two teaspoonsful of sugar in my coffee.'

"I'll look that up,' the girl at Lattimore said, overhearing Myra. She turned to her files.

'What I want to find out,' Tito said to her, 'is the exact date at which the organ was obtained from the UN's VOFR. If you can give me that datum, please.' He waited, accustomed to having to be patient. His line of work absolutely required that virtue, above all others, including intelligence.

The girl presently said, 'A Colonel Weiswasser received an organ transplant on August twelve of this year. Islands of Langerhans, obtained from the VOFR the day before, August eleven. Dr Lurton Sands performed the operation and of course certified the organ.'

'Thanks, miss,' Tito said, and broke the connection. 'The VOFR office is closed,' Myra said, as he began once more to dial. 'You'll have to wait until tomorrow.'

'I know somebody there,' Tito said and continued dialing.

At last he had Gus Anderton, his contact at the UN's vital organ bank. 'Gus, this is Tito. Check August eleven this year for me. Islands of Langerhans; okay? See if the org-trans surgeon we previously had reference to picked up one there on that date.'

His contact was back almost at once with the information. 'Correct, Tito; it all checks out. Aug eleven, Islands of Langerhans. Transferred by jet-hopper to Lattimore in San Francisco. Routine in every way.'

Tito Cravelli cut the circuit, exasperated.

After a pause Myra Sands, still pacing restlessly about his office, exclaimed, 'But I *know* he's been obtaining organs illegally. He never turned anybody down, and you know there never have been that many organs in the bank reserve — he had to get them somewhere else. He still is; I know it.'

'Knowing this and proving this are two . . .'

Turning to him, Myra snapped, 'And outside of the UN bank there's only one other place he would or could go.'

'Agreed,' Tito said, nodding. 'But as your attorney said, you better have proof before you make the charge; otherwise he'll sue you for slander, libel, defamation of character, the entire biz. He'd have to. You'd give him no choice.'

'You don't like this,' Myra said.

Tito shrugged. 'I don't have to like it. That doesn't matter.'

'But you think I'm treading on dangerous ground.'

'I know you are. Even if it's true that Lurton Sands . . .'

'Don't say "even if." He's a fanatic and you know it; he identifies so fully with his public image as a savior of lives that he's simply had to make a psychological break with reality. Probably he started in a small way, with what he told himself was a unique situation, an exception; he had to have a particular organ and he took it. And the next time . . .' She shrugged. 'It was easier. And so on.'

'I see,' Tito said.

'I think I see what we're going to have to do,' Myra said. 'What *you're* going to have to do. Get started on this. Find out from your contact at the UN exactly what organ the bank lacks at this time. Then deliberately set up another emergency situation; have someone in a hospital somewhere apply to Lurton for that particular transplant. I realize that it'll cost one hell of a lot of money, but I'm willing to underwrite the expense. Do you see?'

'I see,' Tito said. In other words, trap Lurton Sands. Play on the man's determination to save the life of a dying person . . . make his humanitarianism the instrument of his destruction. What a way to earn a living, Tito thought to himself. Another day, another dollar . . . it's hardly that. Not when you get involved in something like this.

'I know you can arrange it,' Myra said to him fervently. 'You're good; you're experienced. Aren't you?'

'Yes, Mrs Sands,' Tito said. 'I'm experienced. Yes, possibly I can trap the guy. Lead him by the nose. It shouldn't be too hard.'

'Make sure your "patient" offers him plenty,' Myra said in a bitter, taut voice. 'Lurton will bite if he senses a good financial return; that's what interests him — in spite of what you and the darn public may or may not imagine. I ought to know; I've lived with him a good many years, shared his most intimate thoughts.' She smiled, briefly. 'It seems a shame I have to tell you how to go about your business, but obviously I have to.' Her smile returned, cold and exceedingly hard.

'I appreciate your assistance,' Tito said woodenly.

'No you don't. You think I'm trying to do something wicked. Something out of mere spite.'

Tito said, 'I don't think anything; I'm just hungry. Maybe you don't eat until eight-thirty or nine, but I have pyloric spasms and I have to eat by seven. Will you excuse me?' He rose to his feet, pushing his desk chair back. 'I want to close up shop.' He did not renew his offer to take her out to dinner.

Gathering up her coat and purse, Myra Sands said, 'Have you located Cally Vale and if so where?'

'No luck,' Tito said, and felt uncomfortable.

Staring at him, Myra said, 'But why can't you locate her? She must be *somewhere!*' She looked as if she could not believe her ears.

'The court process servers can't find her either,' Tito pointed out. 'But I'm sure she'll turn up by trial time.' He, too, had been wondering why his staff had been unable to locate Lurton Sands' mistress; after all, there were only a limited number of places a person could hide, and detection and tracing devices, especially during the last two decades, had improved to an almost supernatural accuracy.

Myra said, 'I'm beginning to think you're just not any good. I wonder if I shouldn't put my business in somebody else's hands.'

'That's your privilege,' Tito said. His stomach ached, a series of spasms of his pyloric valve. He wondered if he was ever going to get an opportunity to eat tonight.

'You must find Miss Vale,' Myra said. 'She knows all the details of his activity; that's why he's got her hidden — in fact she's pumping blood with a heart he procured for her.'

'Okay, Mrs Sands,' Tito agreed, and inwardly winced at the growing pain . . .

4

THE BLACK-HAIRED, EXTREMELY dark youth said shyly, 'We came to you, Mrs Sands, because we read about you in the homeopape. It said you were very good and also you take people without too much money.' He added, 'We don't have any money at all right now, but maybe we can pay you later.'

Brusquely, Myra Sands said, 'Don't worry about that now.' She surveyed the boy and girl. 'Let's see. Your names are Art and Rachael Chaffy. Sit down, both of you, and let's talk, all right?' She smiled at them, her professional smile of greeting and warmth; it was reserved for her clients, given to no one else, not even to her husband — or, as she thought of Lurton now, her former husband.

In a soft voice the girl, Rachael, said 'We tried to get them to let us become bibs but they said we should consult an advisor first.' She explained, 'I'm — well, you see, somehow I got to be preg. I'm sorry.' She ducked her head fearfully, with shame, her cheeks flushing deep scarlet. 'It's too bad they don't just let you kill yourself, like they did a few years ago,' she murmured. 'Because that would solve it.'

'That law,' Myra said firmly, 'was a bad idea. However imperfect deep-sleep is, it's certainly preferable to the old form of self-destruction undertaken on an individual basis. How far advanced is your pregnancy, dear?'

'About a month and a half,' Rachael Chaffy said, lifting her head a trifle. She managed to meet Myra's gaze; for a moment, at least.

'Then abort-processing presents no difficulty,' Myra said. 'It's routine. We can arrange for it by noon today and have it done by six tonight. At any one of several free government abort clinics here in the area. Just a moment.' Her secretary had opened the door to the office and was trying to catch her attention. 'What is it, Tina?'

'An urgent phone call for you, Mrs Sands.'

Myra clicked on her desk vidphone. On the screen Tito Cravelli's features formed in replica, puffy with agitation.

'Mrs Sands.' Tito said, 'sorry to bother you at your office so early this morning. But a number of tracking devices we've been employing here have wound up their term of service and have come home. I thought you'd want to know. Cally Vale is nowhere on Earth. That's absolutely been determined; that's definite.' He was silent, then, waiting for her to say something.

'Then she emigrated,' Myra said, trying to picture the dainty and rather nauseatingly fragile Miss Vale in the rugged environment of Mars or Ganymede.

'No,' Tito Cravelli said emphatically, shaking his head. 'We've checked on that, of course. *Cally Vale did not emigrate.* It doesn't make sense, but there it is. No wonder we're making no headway; we're faced with an impossible situation.' He did not appear very happy about it. His features sagged glumly.

Myra said, 'She's not on Earth and she didn't emigrate. Then she must . . .' It was obvious to her; why hadn't they thought of it right away, when Cally originally vanished from sight? 'She's entered a government warehouse. Cally's a bib.' It was the only possibility left.

'We're looking into that,' Tito said, but without enthusiasm. 'I admit it's possible but frankly I just don't buy it Personally, I think they've thought up something new, something original; I'd stake my job on it, everything I have.' Tito's tone was insistent, now. No longer hesitant. 'But we'll check all the Dept. of SPW warehouses, all ninety-four of them. That'll take a couple of days at least. Meanwhile —' He caught sight of the young couple, the Chaffys, waiting silently. 'Perhaps I'd better discuss it with you later; there's no urgency.'

Maybe what the homeopapes are hinting at actually did take place, Myra thought to herself. Perhaps Lurton has actually killed her. So she can't be subpoenaed by Frank Fenner at the trial.

'Do you believe Cally Vale is dead?' Myra said to Tito bluntly. She ignored the young couple seated opposite her; they did not at the moment matter: this was far too important.

'I'm in no position . . .' Tito began. Myra cut him off; she broke the connection, and the screen faded. I'm in no position to say, she finished for him. But who is? Lurton? Maybe even he doesn't know where Cally is. She might have run out on him. Gone to the Golden Door Moments of Bliss satellite and joined the army of girls there, under an assumed name. With relish, Myra pondered that, picturing her former husband's mistress as one of Thisbe's creatures, sexless and mechanical and automatic. Which will it be, Cally? One, two, three or four? Only, the choice isn't yours. It's theirs. Every time. Myra laughed. It's where you ought to be, Cally, she thought. For the rest of your life, for the next two hundred years.

'Please forgive the interruption,' Myra said to the young couple seated opposite her. 'And do go on.'

'Well,' the girl Rachael said awkwardly, 'Art and I felt that — we thought over the abortion and we just don't want to do it. I don't know why, Mrs Sands. I know we should. But we can't.'

There was silence, then.

'I don't see what you came to me for,' Myra said. 'If you've made up your minds against it already. Obviously, from a practical standpoint you should go through with it; you're probably frightened . . . after all, you are very young. But I'm not trying to talk you into it. A decision of this sort has to be your own.'

In a low voice Art said, 'We're not scared, Mrs Sands. That's not it. We — well, we'd like to have the baby. That's all.'

Myra Sands did not know what to say. She had never, in her practice, run into anything quite like this; it baffled her.

She could see already that this was going to be a bad day. Between this and Tito's phonecall — it was too much. And so early. It was not yet even nine A.M.

In the basement of Pethel Jiff-scuttler Sales & Service, the repairman Rick Erickson prepared, for the second day in a row, to enter the defective 'scuttler of Dr Lurton Sands, Jr. He still had not found what he was searching for.

However, he did not intend to give up. He felt, on an intuitive level, that he was very close. It would not be long now.

From behind him a voice said, 'What are you doing, Rick?'

Startled, Erickson jumped, glanced around. At the door of the repair department stood his employer, Darius Pethel, heavy-set in the wrinkled dark-brown old-fashioned *jerry*-type wool suit which he customarily wore.

'Listen,' Erickson said. This is Dr Sands' 'scuttler. You can laugh, but I think he's got his mistress in here, somewhere.'

'What?' Pethel laughed.

'I mean it. I don't think she's dead, even though I talked to Sands long enough to know he could do it if he felt it was necessary — he's that kind of guy. Anyhow nobody's found her, even Mrs Sands. Naturally they can't find her, because Lurton's got his 'scuttler in here with us, out of sight. He knows it's here, *but they don't.* And he doesn't want it back, no matter what he says; he wants it stuck down here, right in this basement.'

Staring at him Pethel said, 'Great fud. Is this what you've been doing on my time? Working out detective theories?'

Erickson said, 'This is important! Even if it doesn't mean any money for you. Hell, maybe it does; if I'm lucky and find her, maybe you can sell her back to Mrs Sands.'

After a pause Darius Pethel shrugged in a philosophical way. 'Okay. So look. If you do find her — '

Beside Pethel the salesman of the firm, Stuart Hadley, appeared. He said breezily, 'What's up, Dar?' As always cheerful and interested.

'Rick's searching for Dr Sands' mistress,' Pethel said. He jerked his thumb at the 'scuttler.

'Is she pretty?' Hadley asked. 'Well started?' He looked hungry.

'You've seen her pics in the homeopapes,' Pethel said. 'She's cute. Otherwise why do you suppose the doctor risked his marriage, if she wasn't something exceptional? Come on, Hadley; I need you upstairs on the floor. We can't all three be down here — someone'll walk away with the register.' He started up the stairs.

'And she's in there?' Hadley said, looking puzzled as he bent to peer into the 'scuttler. 'I don't see her, Dar.'

Darius Pethel gaffawed. 'Neither do I. Neither does Rick, but he's still searching — and on my time, goddam it! Listen, Rick; if you find her she's *my* mistress, because you're on my time, working for me.'

All three of them laughed at that.

'Okay,' Rick agreed, on his hands and knees, scraping the surface of the 'scuttler tube with the blade of a screwdriver. 'You can laugh and I admit it's funny. But I'm not stopping. Obviously, the rent isn't visible; if it was, Doc Sands wouldn't have dared leave it here. He may think I'm dumb, but not that dumb — he's got it concealed and real well.'

'"Rent,"' Pethel echoed. He frowned, starting back a few steps down the stairs and into the basement once more. 'You mean like Henry Ellis found, years ago? That rupture in the tube-wall that led to ancient Israel?'

'Israel is right,' Rick said briefly, as he scraped. His keen, thoroughly-trained eye saw all at once in the surface near at hand a slight irregularity, a distortion. Leaning forward, he reached out his hand . . .

His groping fingers passed through the wall of the tube and disappeared.

'Jesus,' Rick said. He raised his invisible fingers, felt nothing at first, and then touched the upper edge of the rent. 'I found it,' he said. He looked around, but Pethel had gone. 'Darius!' he yelled, but there was no answer. 'Damn him!' he said in fury to Hadley.

'You found what?' Hadley asked, starting cautiously into the tube. 'You mean you found the Vale woman? Cally Vale?'

Headfirst, Rick Erickson crept into the rent.

He sprawled, snatching for support; falling, he struck hard ground and cursed. Opening his eyes, he saw, above, a pale blue sky with a few meager clouds. And, around him, a meadow. Bees, or what looked something more or less like bees, buzzed in tall-stemmed white flowers as large as saucers. The air smelled of sweetness, as if the flowers had impregnated the atmosphere itself.

I'm there, he said to himself. I got through; this is where Doc Sands hid his mistress to keep her from testifying for Mrs Sands at the trial or hearing or whatever it's called. He stood up, cautiously. Behind him he made out a hazy shimmer: the nexus with the tube of the Jiffi-scuttler back in the store's basement in Kansas City. I want to keep my bearings, he said to himself warily. If I get lost, I may not be able to get back again and that might be bad.

Where is this? he asked himself. Must work that out — now.

Gravity like Earth's. Must be Earth, then, he decided. Long time ago? Long time in the future? Think what this is worth; the hell with the man's mistress, the hell with him and his personal problems — that's nothing. He looked wildly around for some sign of habitation, for something animal-like, or human; something to tell him what epoch this was, past or future. Saber-tooth tiger, maybe. Or trilobite. No, too late for the trilobite already; look at those bees. This is the break Terran Development has been trying to uncover for thirty years now, he said to himself. And the rat that found it used it for his own sneaky goings-on, as a place merely to hide his doxie. What a world! Erickson began slowly to walk, step by step . . .

Far off, a figure moved.

Shading his eyes against the glare of the sky, Rick Erickson tried to make out what it was. Primitive man? Cro-Magnon or some such thing? Big-domed inhabitant of the future, perhaps? He squinted — it was a woman; he could tell by her hair. She wore slacks and she was running toward him. Cally, he thought. Doc Sands' mistress, hurrying toward me. Must think I'm Sands. In panic, he halted; what'll I do? he wondered. Maybe I better go back, think this out. He started to turn in the direction he had come.

Out of the corner of his eye he saw the girl's arm come up swiftly.

No, he thought. Don't.

He stumbled as he snatched at the hazy, small loop which connected the two environments, entrance to the 'scuttler tube.

The red glow of an aimed laser-beam passed over his head.

You missed me, he thought in terror. But — he clawed for the entrance, found it, began to struggle back through. But next time. *Next time!*

'Stop,' he shouted at her without looking at her. His voice echoed in the bee-zooming plain of flowers.

The second laser-beam caught him in the back.

He put his hand out, saw it pass through the haze and disappear beyond. It was safe, but he was not. She had killed him; it was too late, now, too late to get away from her. Why didn't she wait? he asked himself. Find out who I was? Must have been afraid.

Again the laser-beam flicked. It touched the back of his head and that was that. There was no returning for him, no reentry into the safety of the tube.

Rick Erickson was dead.

Standing on the far side, in the tube of Dr Sands' Jiffi-scuttler, Stuart Hadley waited nervously, then saw Rick Erickson's fingers jerk through the wall near the floor; the fingers writhed, and Hadley stooped down and grabbed Erickson by the wrist. Trying to get back, he realized, and pulled Erickson by the arm with all his strength.

It was a corpse that he drew into the tube beside him.

Horrified, Hadley rose unsteadily to his feet; he saw the two clean holes and knew that Erickson had been killed with a laser rifle, probably from a distance. Stumbling down the tube, Hadley reached the controls of the 'scuttler and cut the power off; the shimmer of the entrance hoop at once vanished, and he knew or hoped — that now they, whoever they were who had murdered Rick Erickson, could not follow him through.

'Pethel!' he shouted. 'Come down here!' He ran to Erickson's work bench and the intercom. 'Mr Pethel,' he said, 'come back down here to the basement right away. Erickson's dead.'

The next he knew, Darius Pethel stood beside him, examining the body of the repairman. 'He must have found it,' Pethel muttered, ashen-faced and trembling. 'Well, he got paid for his nosiness; he sure got paid.'

'We better get the police,' Hadley said.

'Yes.' Pethel nodded vacantly. 'Of course. I see you turned it off. Good thing. We better leave it strictly alone. The poor guy, the poor goddam guy; look at what he got for being smart enough to figure it all out. Look, he's got something in his hand.' He bent down, opening Erickson's fingers.

The dead hand held a wad of grass.

'No org-trans operation can help him, either,' Pethel said. 'Because the beam caught him in the head. Got his brain. Too bad.' He glanced at Stuart Hadley. 'Anyhow the best org-trans surgeon is Sands and he isn't going to do anything to help Erickson. You can make book on that.'

'A place where there's grass,' Hadley murmured, touching the contents of the dead man's hand. 'Where can it be? Not on Earth. Not now, anyway.'

'Must be the past,' Pethel said. 'So we've got time-travel. Isn't it great?' His face twisted with grief. 'Terrific beginning, one good man dead. How many left to go? Imagine a guy's reputation meaning that much to him, that he'd let this happen. Or maybe Sands doesn't know; maybe she was just given the laser gun to protect herself. In case his wife's private cops got to her. And anyhow, we don't know for sure if she did it; it could have been someone else entirely, not Cally Vale at all. What do we know about it? All we know is that Erickson is dead. And there was something basically wrong with the theory he was going on.'

'You can give Sands the benefit of the doubt, if you want,' Hadley said, 'but I'm not going to.' He stood up, then, taking a deep shuddering breath. 'Can we get the police, now? You call them; I can't talk well enough to. You do it, Pethel, okay?'

Unsteadily, Darius Pethel moved toward the phone on Erickson's work bench, his hand extended gropingly, as if his apperception of touch had begun to disintegrate. He picked up the receiver, and then he turned to Stuart Hadley and said, 'Wait. This is a mistake. You know who we've got to call? The factory. We have to tell Terran Development about this; it's what they're after. They come first.'

Hadley, staring at him, said, 'I — don't agree.'

'This is more important than what you think or I think, more important than Sands and Cally Vale, any of us.' Dar Pethel began to dial. 'Even if one of us is dead. That still doesn't matter. You know what I'm thinking about? Emigration. You saw the grass in Erickson's hand. You know what it means. It means the hell with that girl on the far side, or whoever it is over there who shot Erickson. It means the hell with any of us and all of us, our sentiments and opinions.' He gestured. 'All our lives put together.'

Dimly, Stuart Hadley understood. Or thought he did. 'But she'll probably kill the next person who . . .'

'Let TD worry about that,' Pethel said savagely. 'That's their problem. They've got company police, armed guards they use for patrol purposes; let them send them over, first.' His voice was low and harsh. 'Let them lose a few men, so what. The lives of millions of people are involved in this, now. You get that, Hadley? *Do you?*'

'Y-yes,' Hadley said, nodding.

'Anyhow,' Pethel said, more calmly, now, 'it's legitimately within the jurisdiction of TD because it took place within one of their 'scuttlers. Call it an accident; think of it that way. Unavoidable and awful. Between an entrance and an exit hoop.

Naturally the company has to know.' He turned his back to Hadley, then, concentrating on the vid-phone, calling Leon Turpin, the chief of TD.

'I think,' Salisbury Heim said to his presidential candidate James Briskin, 'I have something cooking you won't like. I've been talking to George Walt . . .'

At once Jim Briskin said, 'No deal. Not with them. I know what they want and that's out, Sal.'

'If you don't do business with George Walt,' Heim said steadily, 'I'm going to have to resign as your campaign manager. I just can't take any more, not after that planet-wetting speech of yours. Things are breaking too badly for us as it is, we can't take George Walt on in addition to everything else.'

'There's something even worse,' Jim Briskin said, after a pause. 'Which you haven't heard. A wire came from Bruno Mini. He was delighted with my speech and he's on his way here to — as he puts it — "join forces with me."'

Heim said, 'But you can still . . .'

'Mini's already spoken to homeopape reporters. So it's too late to head him off media-wise. Sorry.'

'You're going to lose.'

'Okay, I'll have to lose.'

'What gets me,' Heim said bitterly, 'what really gets me is that even if you did win the election you couldn't have it all your way; one man just can't alter things that much. The Golden Door Movements of Bliss satellite is going to remain; the bibs are going to remain; so are Nonovulid and the abort-consultants you can chip away a little here and there but not . . .'

He ceased, because Dorothy Gill had come up to Jim Briskin. 'A phone call for you, Mr Briskin. The gentleman says it's urgent and he won't be wasting your time. You don't know him, he says, so he didn't give his name.' She added, 'He's a Col. If that helps you identify him.'

'It doesn't,' Jim said. 'But I'll talk to him anyhow.' Obviously, he was glad to break off the conversation with Sal; relief showed on his face. 'Bring the phone here, Dotty.'

'Yes, Mr Briskin.' She disappeared and presently was back, carrying the extension vidphone.

'Thanks.' Jim Briskin pressed the hold button, releasing it, and the vidscreen glowed. A face formed, swarthy and hand-some, a keen-eyed man, well-dressed and evidently agitated. Who is he? Sal Heim asked himself. I know him. I've seen a pic of him somewhere.

Then he identified the man. It was the big-time N'York inves-tigator who was working for Myra Sands; it was a man named Tito Cravelli, and he was a tough individual indeed. What did he want with Jim?

The image of Tito Cravelli said, 'Mr Briskin, I'd like to have lunch with you. In private. I have something to discuss with you, just you and me; it's vitally important to you, I assure you.' He added, with a glance toward Sal Heim, 'So vital I don't want anybody else around.'

Maybe this is going to be an assassination attempt, Sal Heim thought. Someone, a fanatic from CLEAN, sent by Verne Engel and his crowd of nuts. 'You better not go, Jim,' he said aloud.

'Probably not,' Jim said. 'But I am anyhow.' To the image on the vidscreen he said, 'What time and where?'

Tito Cravelli said, 'There's a little restaurant in the N'York slum area, in the five hundred block of Fifth Avenue; I always eat there when I'm in N'York — the food's prepared by hand. It's called Scotty's Place. Will that be satisfactory? Say at one P.M., N'York time.'

'All right,' Jim Briskin agreed. 'At Scotty's Place at one o'clock.

I've been there.' He added tartly, 'They're willing to serve Cols.'

'Everyone serves Cols,' Tito said, 'when I'm along.' He broke the connection; the screen faded and died.

'I don't like this,' Sal Heim said.

'We're ruined anyhow,' Jim reminded him. 'Didn't you say, just a minute ago?' He smiled laconically. 'I think the time has arrived for me to clutch at straws, Sal. Any straw I can reach. Even this.'

'What shall I tell George Walt? They're waiting. I'm supposed to set up a visit by you to the satellite within twenty-four hours; that would be by six o'clock tonight.' Getting out his handkerchief, Sal Heim mopped his forehead. 'After that. . . .'

'After that,' Jim said, 'they begin systematically campaigning against me.'

Sal nodded.

'You can tell George Walt,' Jim said, 'that in my Chicago speech today I'm going to come out and advocate the shutting of the satellite. And if I'm elected . . .'

'They know already,' Sal Heim said. 'There was a leak.'

'There's always a leak.' Jim did not seem perturbed.

Reaching into his coat pocket, Sal brought out a sealed envelope. 'Here's my resignation.' He had been carrying it for some time.

Jim Briskin accepted the envelope; without opening it he put it in his coat-pouch. 'I hope you'll be watching my Chicago speech. Sal. It's going to be an important one.' He grinned sorrowfully at his ex-campaign manager; his pain at this break-down of their relationship showed in the deep lines of his face. The break had been long in coming; it had hung there in the atmosphere between them in their former discussions.

But Jim intended to go on anyhow. And do what had to be done.

5

As HE FLEW by Jet'ab to Scotty's Place, Jim Briskin thought: At least now I don't have to come out for Lurton Sands; I don't have to follow Sal's advice any more on any topic because if he's not my campaign manager he can't tell me what to do. To some extent it was a relief. But on a deeper level Jim Briskin felt acutely unhappy. I'm going to have trouble getting along without Sal, he realized. I don't *want* to get along without him.

But it was already done. Sal, with his wife Patricia, had gone on to his home in Cleveland, for a much-delayed rest. And Jim Briskin, with his speech writer Phil Danville and his press secretary Dorothy Gill, was on his way in the opposite direction, toward downtown N'York, its tiny shops and restaurants and old, decaying apartment buildings, and all the microscopic, outdated business offices where peculiar and occult transactions continually took place. It was a world which intrigued Jim Briskin, but it was also a world he knew little about; he had been shielded from it most of his life.

Seated beside him, Phil Danville said, 'He may come back, Jim. You know Sal when he gets overburdened; he blows up, falls into fragments. But after a week of lazing around . . .'

'Not this time,' Jim said. The split was too basic.

'By the way,' Dorothy said, 'before he left, Sal told me who this man you're meeting is. Sal recognized him; did he tell you? It's Tito Cravelli, Sal says. You know, Myra Sands' investigator.'

'No,' Jim said. 'I didn't know.' Sal had said nothing to him; the period in which Sal Heim gave him the benefit of his experience was over, had ended there on the spot.

At Republican-Liberal campaign headquarters in N'York he stopped briefly to let off Phil Danville and Dorothy Gill, and then he went on, alone, to meet with Tito Cravelli at Scotty's Place.

Cravelli, looking nervous and keyed-up, was already in a booth in the rear of the restaurant, waiting for him, when he arrived.

'Thanks, Mr Briskin,' Tito Cravelli said, as Jim seated himself across from him. Hurriedly, Cravelli sipped what remained of his cup of coffee. 'This won't take long. What I want for my information is a great deal. I want a promise from you that when you're elected — and you will be, because of this — you'll bring me in at cabinet rank.' He was silent, then.

'Good god,' Jim said mildly. 'Is that all you want?'

'I'm entitled to it,' Cravelli said. 'For getting this information to you. I came across it because I have someone working for me in . . .' He broke off abruptly. 'I want the post of Attorney General; I think I can handle the job . . . I think I'll be a good Attorney General. If I'm not, you can fire me. But you have to let me in for a chance at it.'

'Tell me what your information is. I can't make that promise until I hear it.'

Cravelli hesitated. 'Once I tell you — but you're honest, Briskin. Everyone knows that. There's a way you can get rid of the bibs. You can bring them back to activity, full activity.'

'Where?'

'Not here,' Cravelli said. 'Obviously. Not on Earth. The man I have working for me who picked this up is an employee of Terran Development. What does that suggest to you?'

After a pause Jim Briskin said, 'They've made a breakthrough.'

'A little firm has. A retailer in Kansas City, repairing a defective Jiffi-scuttler. They did it — or rather found it. Discovered it. The 'scuttler's at TD, now, being gone over by factory engineers. It was moved east two hours ago; they acted immediately, as soon as the retailer contacted them. They knew what it meant.' He added, 'Just as you and I do, and my man working for them.'

'Where's the breakthrough to? What time period?'

'No time period, evidently. The conversion seems to have taken place in spacial terms, as near as they can determine. A planet with about the same mass as Earth, similar atmosphere, well-developed fauna and flora, but not Earth — they managed to snap a sky-chart, get a stellar reading. Within another few hours they'll probably have plotted it exactly, know which starsystem it lies in. Apparently it's a long, long way from here. Too far for direct deepspace ships to probe — at least for some time to come. This breakthrough, this direct shorted-out route, will have to be utilized for at least the next few decades.'

The waitress came for Jim's order.

'Perkin's Syn-Cof,' he murmured absently.

The waitress departed.

'Cally Vale's there,' Tito Cravelli said.

'What!'

'Doctor put her across. That's why my man got in touch with me; as you may know, I've been retained to search for Cally, trying to produce her on demand for the trial. It's a mess; she lasered an employee of this Kansas City retailer, its one and only tried and true 'scuttler repairman. He had gone across, exploring. Too bad for him. But in the great scheme of all things . . .'

'Yes,' Jim Briskin agreed. Cravelli was right; it was small

cost indeed. With so many millions of lives — and, potentially, billions — involved.

'Naturally TD has declared this top-secret. They've thrown up an enormous security screen; I was lucky to get hold of the poop at all. If I hadn't already had a man in there . . .' Cravelli gestured.

'I'll name you to the cabinet,' Jim Briskin said. 'As Attorney General. The arrangement doesn't please me, but I think it's in order.' It's worth it, he said to himself. A hundred times over. To me and to everyone else on Earth, bibs and non-bibs alike. To all of us.

Sagging with relief and exultation, Tito Cravelli burbled, 'Wow. I can't believe it; this is great!' He held out his hand, but Jim ignored it; he had too much else on his mind at the moment to want to congratulate Tito Cravelli.

Jim thought, *Sal Heim got out a little too soon. He should have stuck around.* So much for Sal's political intuition; at the crucial moment it had failed to materialize for him.

Seated in her office, abort-consultant Myra Sands once more leafed through Tito's brief report. But already, outside her window, a news machine for one of the major homeopapes was screeching out the news that Cally Vale had been found; it had been made public by the police.

I didn't think you could do it, Tito, Myra said to herself. Well, I was wrong. You were worth your fee, large as it is.

It will be quite a trial, she said to herself with relish.

From a nearby office, probably the brokerage firm next door, the amplified sound of a man's voice rose up and then was turned down to a more reasonable level. Someone had tuned in the TV, was watching the Republican-Liberal presidential candidate giving his latest speech. Perhaps I should listen, too, she decided, and reached to turn on the TV set at her desk.

The set warmed, and there, on the screen, appeared the dark, intense features of Jim Briskin. She swiveled her chair toward the set and momentarily put aside Tito's report. After all, anything James Briskin said had become important; he might easily be their next president.

'. . . an initial action on my part,' Briskin was saying, 'and one which many may disapprove of, but one dear to my heart, will be to initiate legal action against the so-called Golden Door Moments of Bliss satellite. I've thought about this topic for some time; this is not a snap decision on my part. But, much more vital than that, I think we will see the Golden Door satellite become thoroughly obsolete. That would be best of all. The role of sexuality in our society could return to its biological norm: as a means to childbirth rather than an end in itself.'

Oh, really? Myra thought archly. Exactly how?

'I am about to give you a piece of news which none of you have heard,' Briskin continued. 'It will make a vast difference in all our lives . . . so great, in fact, that no one could possibly foresee its full extent at this time. A new possibility for emigration is about to open up at last. At Terran Development . . .'

On Myra's desk the vidphone rang. Cursing in irritation, she turned down the sound of the television set and took the receiver from its support. 'This is Mrs Sands,' she said. 'Could you please call back in a few moments, thank you? I'm extremely busy right now.'

It was the dark-haired boy, Art Chaffy. 'We were just wondering what you'd decided,' he mumbled apologetically. But he did not ring off. 'It means a lot to us, Mrs Sands.'

'I know it does, Art,' Myra Sands said, 'but if you'll just give me a few more minutes, possibly half an hour . . .' She strained to hear what James Briskin was saying on the television; almost, she could make out the low murmur of words. What was his new news? Where were they going to emigrate to? A virgin environment? Well, obviously; it would have to be. But precisely where is it? Myra wondered. Are you about to pull this virgin world out of your sleeve, Mr Briskin? Because if you are, I would like to see it done; that would be worth watching.

'Okay,' Art Chaffy said. 'I'll call you later, Mrs Sands. And I'm sorry to pester you.' He rang off, then.

'You ought to be listening to Briskin's speech,' Myra murmured aloud as she swung her chair back to face the television set; bending, she turned the audio knob and the sound of Briskin's voice rose once more to clear audibility. You of all people, she said to herself.

'. . . and according to reports reaching me,' Briskin said slowly and gravely, 'it has an atmosphere nearly identical to that of earth, and a similar mass as well.'

Good grief, Myra Sands said to herself. If that's the case then I'm out of a job. Her heart labored painfully. No one would need abort brokers any more. But frankly I'm just as glad, she decided. It's a task I'd like to see end — forever.

Hands pressed together tautly, she listened to the remainder of Jim Briskin's momentous Chicago speech.

My god, she thought. This is a piece of history being made, this discovery. If it's true. If this isn't just a campaign stunt.

Somewhere inside her she knew that it was true. Because Jim Briskin was not the kind of person who would make this up.

At the Oakland, California, branch of the U.S. Government Department of Special Public Welfare, Herbert Lackmore also sat listening to presidential candidate Jim Briskin's Chicago speech, being carried on all channels of the TV as it was beamed from the R-L satellite above.

He'll be elected now, Lackmore realized. We'll have a Col president at last, just what I was afraid of.

And, if what he's saying is so, this business about a new possibility of emigration to an untouched world with fauna and flora like Earth's, it means the bibs will be awakened. In fact, he realized with a thrill of fright, it means there won't be any more bibs. At all.

That would mean that Herb Lackmore's job would come to an end. And right away.

Because of him, Lackmore said to himself, I'm going to be out of work; I'll be in the same spot as all the Cols who come by here in a steady stream, day in day out — I'll be like some nine-teen-year-old Mexican or Puerto Rican or Negro kid, without prospects or hope. All I've established over the years — wiped out by this. Completely.

With shaking fingers, Herb Lackmore opened the local phone book and turned the pages.

It was time to get hold of — and join — the organization of Verne Engel's which called itself CLEAN. Because CLEAN would not sit idly by and let this happen, not if CLEAN believed as Herb Lackmore did.

Now was the time for CLEAN to do something. And not necessarily of a non-violent nature; it was too late for non-violence to work. Something more was required, now. Much more. The situation had taken a dreadful turn and it would have to be rectified, by direct and quick action.

And if they won't do it, Lackmore said to himself, I will. I'm not afraid to; I know it has to be done.

On the TV screen Jim Briskin's face was stern as he said, '. . . will provide a natural outlet for the biological pressures at work on everyone in our society. We will be free at last to . . .'

'You know what this means?' George of George Walt said to his brother Walt.

'I know,' Walt answered. 'It means that nurf Sal Heim got nothing for us, nothing at all. You watch Briskin; I'm going to call Verne Engel and make some kind of arrangements. Him we can work with.'

'Okay,' George said, nodding their shared head. He kept his eye on the TV screen, while his brother dialed the vidphone.

'All that gabble with Sal Heim,' Walt grumbled, and then became silent as his brother stuck him with his elbow, signaling that he wanted to listen to the Chicago speech. 'Sorry,' Walt said, turning his eye to the vidscreen of the phone.

At the door of their office Thisbe Olt appeared, wearing a fawnskin gown with alternating stripes of magnifying transparency. 'Mr Heim is back,' she informed them. 'To see you. He looks — dejected.'

'We've got no business to conduct with Sal Heim,' George said, with anger.

'Tell him to go back to Earth,' Walt added. 'And from now on the satellite is closed to him; he can't visit any of our girls — at any price. Let him die a miserable, lingering death of frustration; it'll serve him right.'

George reminded him acidly, 'Heim won't need us any more, if Briskin is telling the truth.'

'He is,' Walt said. 'He's too simple a horse's ass to lie; Briskin doesn't have the ability.' His call had been put through on the private circuit, now. On the vidscreen appeared the miniature image of one of Verne Engel's gaudily-uniformed personal praetorian flunkies, the green and silver outfit of the CLEAN people. 'Let me talk directly to Verne,' Walt said, making use of their common mouth just as George was about to address a few more remarks to Thisbe. 'Tell him this is Walt, on the satellite.'

'Run along,' George said to Thisbe, when Walt had finished. 'We're busy.'

Thisbe eyed him momentarily and then shut the office door after her.

On the screen Verne Engel's pinched, wabble-like face materialized. 'I see you — at least half of you — are following Briskin's rabble-rousing,' Engel said. 'How did you decide which half was to call me and which half was to listen to the Col?' Engel's distorted features twisted in a leer of derision.

'Watch it — that's enough,' George Walt retorted simultaneously.

'Sorry. I don't mean to offend you,' Engel said, but his expression remained unchanged. 'Well, what can I do for you? Please make it brief; I'd like to follow Briskin's harangue too.'

'You're going to require help,' Walt said to Engel. 'If you're going to stop Briskin now; this speech will put him across, and I don't think even concerted transmissions from our satellite — as we discussed — will be sufficient. It's just too damn clever a speech he's making. Isn't it, George?'

'It certainly is,' George said, eye fixed on the TV screen. 'And getting better each second as he goes along. He's barely getting started; it's a genuine spellbinder. Whacking fine.'

His eye on the vidscreen, Walt continued, 'You heard Briskin come out against us; you must have heard that part — everyone else in the country certainly did. Planet-wetting with Bruno Mini isn't enough, he's also got to take us on. Big plans for a Col, but evidently he and his advisors feel he can handle it. We'll see. What do you plan to do, Engel? At this very crucial point?'

'I've got plans, I've got plans,' Engel assured him.

'Still no-violence stuff?'

There was no audible answer, but Engel's face contorted oddly.

'Come up here to the Golden Door,' Walt said, 'and let's talk. I think my brother and I can see our way clear to make a donation to CLEAN, say in the neighborhood of ten or eleven mil. Would that help? You ought to be able to buy what you need with money like that.'

Engel, white with shock, stammered, 'S-sure, George or Walt, whichever you are.'

'Get up here as soon as you can, then,' Walt instructed him, and rang off. 'I think he'll do it for us,' he said to his brother.

'A gorp like that can't handle anything,' George said sourly.

'Then for pop's sake, what do we do?' Walt demanded.

'We do what we can. We help out Engel, we prompt him, shove him if necessary. But we don't pin our hopes on him, at least not entirely. We go ahead with something on our own, just to be certain. And we have to be certain; this is too serious. That Col actually means to shut us down.'

Both their eyes, now, turned toward the TV screen, and both George and Walt sat back in their special wide couch to listen to the speech.

In the luxurious apartment which he maintained in Reno, Dr Lurton Sands sat raptly listening to the television set, the Col candidate James Briskin delivering his Chicago speech. He knew what it meant. There was only one place that Briskin could have happened across a 'lush, virgin world.' Obviously Cally had been found.

Going to his desk drawer, Lurton Sands got out the small laser pistol which he kept there and thrust it into his coat pocket. I'm amazed he'd do it, Sands thought. Capitalize off my problems — evidently I misjudged him.

Now so many lives which I could have saved will be forfeited, Sands realized. Due to this. And Briskin is responsible . . . he's taken the healing power out of my hands, darkened the force working for the good of man.

At the vidphone Sands dialed the local jet'ab company. 'I want an 'ab to Chicago. As soon as possible.' He gave his address, then hurried from his apartment to the elevator. Those that are hounding Cally and me to our deaths, he thought, Myra and her detectives and the homeopapes . . . now they've been joined by Jim Briskin. How could he align himself with them? Haven't I made clear to everyone what I can do in the service of human need? *Briskin must be aware;* this can't be merely ignorance on his part.

Frantically Sands thought. Could it possibly be that Briskin *wants* the sick to die? All those waiting for me, needing my help . . . help which no one else, after I've been pushed to my death, can possibly provide.

Touching the laser pistol in his pocket, Sands said aloud, glumly, 'It certainly is easy to be mistaken about another person.' They can take you in so easily, he thought. Deliberately mislead you. Yes, deliberately!

The jet'ab swept up to the curb and slid open its door.

6

WHEN HE HAD finished his speech Jim Briskin sat back and knew that this time he had done, at last, a damn good job. It had been the best speech of his political career, in some respects the only really decent one.

And now what? he asked himself. Sal is gone, and along with him Patricia. I've offended the powerful and immensely wealthy unicephalic brothers George Walt, not to mention Thisbe herself . . . and Terran Development, which is no small potatoes, will be furious that its break-through has been made public. But none of this matters. Nor does the fact that I'm now committed to naming a well-known private operator as my Attorney General; even that isn't important. My job was to make that speech as soon as Tito Cravelli brought me that information. And — that's exactly what I did. To the letter. No matter what the consequences.

Coming up to him, Phil Danville slapped him warmly on the back. 'A hell of a good fuss, Jim. You really outdid yourself.'

'Thanks, Phil,' Jim Briskin murmured. He felt tired. He nodded to the TV camera men and then, with Phil Danville, walked over to join the knot of party brass waiting at the rear of the studio.

'I need a drink,' Jim said to them as several of them extended their hands, wanting to shake with him. 'After that.' I wonder what the opposition will do now, he said to himself. What can Bill Schwarz say? Nothing, actually. I've taken the lid off the whole thing, and there's no putting it back. Now that everyone knows there's a place we can emigrate to, the rush will be on. By the multitudes. The warehouses will be emptied, thank god. As they should have been long ago.

I wish I had known about this, he thought abruptly, before I began publicly advocating Bruno Mini's planet-wetting technique. I could have avoided that — and the break with Sal as well.

But anyhow, he said to himself, *I'll be elected.*

Dorothy Gill said quietly to him, 'Jim, I think you're in.'

'I know he is,' Phil Danville agreed, grinning with pure delight. 'How about it, Dotty? It's not like it was a little while ago. How'd you get hold of that info about TD, Jim? It must have cost you . . .'

'It did,' Jim Briskin said shortly. 'It cost me too much. But I'd pay it two times over.'

'Now for the drink,' Phil said. 'There's a bar around the corner; I noticed it when we were coming in here. Let's go.' He started for the door and Jim Briskin followed, hands deep in his overcoat pockets.

The sidewalk, he discovered, was crowded with people, a mob which waved at him, cheered him; he waved back, noticing that many of them were Whites as well as Cols. A good sign, he reflected as his party moved step by step through the dense mass of people, uniformed Chicago city police clearing a path for them to the bar which Phil Danville had picked out.

From the crowd a red-headed girl, very small, wearing dazzling wubfur lounging pajamas, the kind fashionable with the girls on the Golden Door Moments of Bliss satellite, came hurrying, gliding and ducking toward him breathlessly. 'Mr Briskin...'

He paused unwillingly, wondering who she was and what she wanted. One of Thisbe Olt's girls, evidently. 'Yes,' he said, and smiled at her.

'Mr Briskin,' the little red-haired girl gasped, 'there's a rume going around the satellite — George Walt's doing something with Verne Engel, the man from CLEAN.' She caught hold of him anxiously by the arm, stopping him. 'They're going to assassinate you or something. Please be careful.' Her face was stark with alarm.

'What's your name?' Jim asked.

'Sparky Rivers. I — work there, Mr Briskin.'

'Thanks, Sparky,' he said. 'I'll remember you. Maybe sometime I can give you a cabinet post.' He continued to smile at her, but she did not smile back. 'I'm just joking,' he said. 'Don't be downcast.'

'I think they're going to kill you,' Sparky said.

'Maybe so.' He shrugged. It was certainly possible. He leaned forward, briefly, and kissed her on the forehead. 'Take care of yourself, too,' he said, and then walked on with Phil Danville and Dorothy Gill.

After a time Phil said, 'What are you going to do, Jim?'

'Nothing. What can I do? Wait, I guess. Get my drink.'

'You'll have to protect yourself,' Dorothy Gill said. 'If anything happens to you — what'll we do then? The rest of us.'

Jim Briskin said, 'Emigration will still exist, even without me. You can still wake the sleepers. As it says in Bach's Cantata 140, *"Wachet auf."* Sleepers, awake. That'll have to be your watchword, from now on.'

'Here's the bar,' Phil Danville said. Ahead of them, a Chicago policeman held the door open for them, and they entered one at a time.

'It was darn nice of that girl to warn me,' Jim Briskin said.

A man's voice, close to him, said, 'Mr Briskin? I'm Lurton Sands, Jr. Perhaps you've been reading about me in the homeo-papes, lately.'

'Oh, yes,' Jim said, surprised to see him; he held out his hand in greeting. 'I'm glad to meet you, Dr Sands. I want to . . .'

'May I talk, please?' Sands said. 'I have something to say to you. Because of you, my life and the humanitarian work of two decades is wrecked. Don't answer; I'm not going to get into an argument with you. I'm simply telling you, so you'll understand why.' Sands reached into his coat pocket. Now he held a laser pistol, pointed directly at Jim Briskin's chest. 'I don't quite un-derstand what it is about my dedication to the sick that offended you and made you turn against me, but everybody else has, so why not you? After all, Mr Briskin, what better life-task could you set yourself than wrecking mine?' He squeezed the trigger of the pistol. The pistol did not fire, and Lurton Sands stared down at it in disbelief. 'Myra, my wife.' He sounded almost apol-ogetic. 'She removed the energy cartridge, obviously. Evidently, she thought I'd try to use it on her.' He tossed the pistol away.

After a pause Jim Briskin said huskily, 'Well, now what, Doc-tor?'

'Nothing, Briskin. Nothing. If I had had more time I would have checked the gun out, but I had to hurry to get here before you left. That was quite a heroic speech you made; it'll certainly give most people the impression that you're seeking to alleviate man's problems . . . although of course you and I know better. By the way — you do realize you won't be able to awaken *all* the bibs; you can't fulfill that promise because some are dead. I'm responsible for that. Roughly four hundred of them.'

Jim Briskin stared at him.

'That's right,' Sands said. 'I've had access to Department of Special Public Welfare warehouses. Do you know what that means? Every organ I've taken has created a dead human — when the time comes for them to be revived, whenever that may be. But I suppose the trump has to be played sooner or later, doesn't it?'

'You'd do that?' Jim Briskin said.

'I *did* that,' Sands corrected. 'But remember this: *I killed only potentially*. Whereas, in exchange, I saved someone right now, someone conscious and alive in the present, someone completely dependent on my skill.'

Two Chicago policemen shoved their way up to him; Dr Sands jerked irritably away but they continued to hold onto him, pinning him between them.

Pale, Phil Danville said, 'That — was almost it, Jim. Wasn't it?' He deliberately stepped between Jim Briskin and Dr Sands, shielding Briskin. 'History revisited.'

'Yes,' Jim managed to say. He nodded, his mouth dry. Basically he felt resigned. If Lurton Sands did not manage to carry it off then, certainly someone else would, given time. It was just too easy. Weapons technology had improved too much in the last hundred years; everyone knew that, and now the assassin did not even have to be in his vicinity. Like an act of evil magic it could be done from a distance. And the instruments were cheap and available to virtually anyone — even, as history had shown, some ignorant, worthless smallfry, without friends, funds, or even a fanatical purpose, an overriding political cause.

This incident with Lurton Sands was a vile harbinger.

'Well,' Phil Danville said, and sighed, 'I guess we have to go on. What do you want to drink?'

'A *Black Russian*,' Jim decided, after a pause. 'Vodka and . . .'

'I know,' Phil interrupted. His face still ragged with fear and gloom, he made his way unsteadily over to the bar to order.

To Dotty, Jim said, 'Even if they get me, I've done my job. I keep telling myself that over and over again, anyhow. I broke the news about TD's breakthrough and that's enough.'

'Do you actually mean that?' she demanded. 'You're that fatalistic about it, about your chances?' She stared unwinkingly up into his face.

'Yes,' he said, finally. And well he might be.

I have a feeling, he thought to himself, that this is not the time a Negro is going to make it to the presidency.

His contact within CLEAN came via an individual named Dave DeWinter. DeWinter had joined the movement at its inception and had reported to Tito Cravelli throughout. Now, hurriedly, DeWinter told his employer the most recent — and urgent — news.

'They'll try it late tonight. The man actually doing it is not a member. His name is Herb Lackmore or Luckmore, and with the equipment they're providing him he doesn't need to be an accurate shot.' DeWinter added, 'The equipment, what they call a *boulder,* was paid for by George Walt, those two mutants who own the Golden Door.'

Tito Cravelli said, 'I see.' There goes my post as Attorney General, he said to himself. 'Where can I find this Lackmore right now?'

'In his conapt in Oakland, California. Probably eating dinner; it's about six, there.'

From the locked closet of his office, Tito Cravelli got a collapsible high-powered scope-sight laser rifle, he folded it up and stuffed it into his pocket, out of sight. Such a rifle was strictly illegal, but that hardly mattered right now; what

Cravelli intended to do was against the law with any kind of weapon.

But it was already too late to get Lackmore or Luckmore or whatever his name was. By the time he reached the West Coast Lackmore would certainly be gone, on his way east to intercept Jim Briskin; their flights would cross, his and Lackmore's. Better to locate Briskin and stick close to him. get Lackmore when he showed up. But Herb Lackmore would not have to show up, in the strict sense, not with the variety of weapon which the mutant brothers had provided him. He could be as far away as ten miles — and still reach Briskin.

George Walt will have to call him off, Cravelli decided. It's the only sure way — and even that is merely *relatively* sure.

I'll have to go to the satellite, he said to himself. Now, if I expect to accomplish anything at all. The mutants George Walt would not be expecting him; they had no knowledge of his ties with Jim Briskin — or so he hoped. And also, he had three individuals working for him on the satellite, three of the girls. That gave him three separate places to stay — or hide — while he was up there. Afterwards, after he took care of George Walt, it might well mean the difference in saving his life.

That, of course, would be if George Walt wouldn't do business with him, if they chose to fight it out. In a fight, they would lose; Tito Cravelli was a crack shot. And in addition the initiative would be with him.

Where was the Golden Door Moments of Bliss satellite right now? Getting the evening homeopape, he turned to the entertainment page. If it was, say, over India, he had no chance; he would not be able to reach the brothers in time.

The Golden Door Moments of Bliss satellite, according to the time-schedule shown in the pape, was right now over Utah. By jet'ab he could reach it within three quarters of an hour.

That was soon enough,

'Thanks a lot,' he said to Dave DeWinter, who stood awkwardly in the middle of the office, wearing his splendid green and silver CLEAN uniform. 'You trot on back to Engel. I'll keep in touch with you.' He left the office on a dead run, then, racing down the stairs to the ground floor.

Presently, he was on his way to the satellite.

When the jet'ab had landed at the field, Cravelli hurried down the ramp, purchased a ticket from the nude, golden-haired attendant, and then rushed through gate five, searching for Francy's door. 705, it was — or so he recalled, but under so much tension he felt rattled. With five thousand doors spread out in corridor after corridor — and all around him, on every side, the animated pics of the girls twisted and chirped, trying to snare his attention and entice him to the joys inside.

I'll have to consult the satellite's directory, he decided. That would waste precious time, but what alternative did he have? Feverishly, he loped down the corridor until he arrived at the immensely extensive, cross-indexed, illuminated directory board, with all its names winking on and off as rooms emptied and refilled, as customers hurried in and out.

It was 507, and it was empty of customers.

When he opened the door Francy said, '*Hello!*' and sat up, then, blinking in surprise to see him. 'Mr Cravelli,' she said uncertainly. 'Is everything all right?' She slid from the bed, wearing a pale smock of some cheap thin material, and came hesitantly up to him, her body bare and smooth. 'What can I do for you? Are you here for . . .'

'Not for pleasure,' Tito Cravelli informed her. 'Button up your damn smock and listen to me. Is there any way you can get George Walt up here?'

Fancy pondered. 'They never visit a crib, normally. I . . .'

'Suppose there was trouble. A customer refusing to pay.'

'No. A bouncer would show up then. But George Walt would

come here if they thought the FBI or some other police agency had moved in here and was officially arresting us girls.' She pointed to an obscure button on the wall. 'For such an emergency. They have a regular neurosis about the police; they think it's bound to come, sooner or later — they must have a guilty conscience about it. The button connects to that great big office of theirs.'

'Ring the button,' Cravelli said, and got out his laser rifle seating himself on Francy's bed, he began to assemble it.

Minutes passed.

Standing uneasily at the door, listening, Francy said 'What's going to happen in here Mr Cravelli? I hope there's no . . .'

'Be quiet,' he said sharply.

The door of the room opened.

The mutants George Walt stood in the entrance, one hand on the knob, the other three gripping short lengths of metal piping.

Tito Cravelli leveled the laser rifle and said, 'My intention is not to kill both of you but merely one of you. That'll leave the other with half a dead brain, one dead eye, and a deteriorating body attached to him. I don't think you'd appreciate that. Can you threaten me with anything equally dreadful? I seriously doubt it.'

After a pause one of them — he did not know which — said, 'What — do you want?' The face was twisting and livid, the two eyes, not in unison, staring, one of them at Tito, the other at his laser rifle.

'Come in and close the door,' Tito Cravelli said.

'Why?' George Walt demanded. 'What's this all about, anyhow?'

'Just come on in,' Tito said, and waited.

The mutants entered. The door shut after them and they stood facing him, still gripping the three lengths of metal piping. 'This is George,' the head said presently. 'Who are you? Let's

be reasonable; if you're dissatisfied with the service you've received from this woman — no, can't you see this is a strong-arm
robbery?' the head interrupted itself as the other brother took
control of the vocal apparatus. 'He's here to rob us; he brought
that weapon with him, didn't he?'

'You're going to get in touch with Verne Engel,' Tito said.
'And he's going to get in touch with his gunsel, Herbert Lackmore. Together you're going to call this Lackmore back in. We'll
do it from your office; obviously we can't call from this woman's
crib.' To Francy he said, 'You go ahead of them, lead the way.
Start now, please. There's no excess of time.' Within him his pyloric valve began to writhe in spasms; he gritted his teeth and
for an instant shut his eyes.

A length of piping whistled past his head.

Tito Cravelli fired the laser rifle at George Walt. One of the
two bodies sagged, hit in the shoulder; it was wounded but not
dead. 'You see?' Cravelli said. 'It would be terrible for the one of
you that survived.'

'Yes,' the head said, bobbing up and down in a grotesque
pumpkin-like fit of nodding. 'We'll work with you, whoever you
are. We'll call Engel; we can get this all straightened out. Please.'
Both eyes, each fixed on a different spot, bulged in glazed fear.
The right one, on the same side as the laser-wound, had become
opaque with pain.

'Good enough,' Tito Cravelli said. He thought, I may be Attorney General yet. Herding them with his laser rifle, he moved
George Walt toward the door.

7

THE WEAPON WHICH Herb Lackmore had been provided with contained a costly replica of the encephalic wave-pattern of James Briskin. He needed merely to place it within a few miles of Briskin, screw in the handle and then, with a switch, detonate it.

It was a mechanism, he decided, which supplied little, if any, personal satisfaction. However, at least it would do the job and that, in the long run, was all that counted. And certainly it insured his personal escape, or at least greatly aided it.

At this moment, nine o'clock at night, Jim Briskin sat upstairs in a room at the Galton Plaza Hotel, in Chicago, conferring with aides and idea-men; pickets of CLEAN, parading before the notably first class hotel, had seen him enter and had conveyed the word to Lackmore.

I'll do it at exactly nine-fifteen, Lackmore decided. He sat in the back of a rented wheel, the mechanism assembled beside him; it was no larger than a football but rather heavy. It hummed faintly, off-key.

I wonder where the funds for this apparatus appeared from, he wondered. Because these items cost a hell of a lot, or so I've read.

He was, a few minutes later, just making the final preparatory adjustments when two dark, massive, upright shapes materialized along the nocturnal sidewalk close beside the wheel. The shapes appeared to be wearing green and silver uniforms which sparkled faintly, like moonlight.

Cautiously, with a near-Psionic sense of suspicions, Lackmore rolled down the wheel window. 'What do you want?' he asked the two CLEAN members.

'Get out,' one of them said brusquely.

'Why?' Lackmore froze, did not budge. Could not.

'There's been an alteration of plans. Engel just now buzzed us on the portable seek-com. You're to give that *boulder* back to us.'

'No,' Lackmore said. Obviously, the CLEAN movement had at the last moment sold out; he did not know exactly why, but there it was. The assassination would not take place as planned — that was all he knew, all he cared about. Rapidly, he began to screw the handle in.

'Engel says to forget it!' the other CLEAN man shouted. 'Don't you understand?'

'I understand,' Lackmore said, and groped for the detonating switch.

The door of his wheel popped open. One of the CLEAN men grabbed him by the collar, yanked him from the back seat and dragged him kicking and thrashing from the wheel and out onto the sidewalk. The other snatched up the *boulder*, the expensive weapon, from him and swiftly, expertly, unscrewed the detonating handle.

Lackmore bit and fought. He did not give up.

It did him no good. The CLEAN man with the *boulder* had already disappeared into the night darkness; along with the weapon he had vanished — the *boulder*, and all of Lackmore's tireless, busy, brooding plans, had gone.

'I'll kill you,' Lackmore panted futilely, struggling with the fat, powerful CLEAN man who had hold of him.

'You'll kill nobody, fella,' the CLEAN man answered, and increased his pressure on Lackmore's throat.

It was not an even fight; Herb Lackmore had no chance. He had sat at a government desk, stood idly behind a counter too many years.

Calmly, with clear enjoyment, the CLEAN man made mincemeat out of him.

For someone supposedly devoted to the cult of non-violence, it was amazing how good he was at it.

From the two mutants' plush, Titan elk-beetle fuzz carpeted office, Tito Cravelli vidphoned Jim Briskin at the Gallon Plaza Hotel in Chicago. 'Are you all right?' he inquired. One of the Golden Door Moments of Bliss satellite's nurses was engaged in attempting futilely to bind up the injured brother with a dermofax pack; she worked silently, as Cravelli held the laser rifle and Francy stood by the office door with a pistol which Tito had located in the brothers' desk.

'I'm all right,' Briskin said, puzzled. He evidently could see around Tito, past him to George Walt.

Tito said, 'I've got a snake by the tail here, and I can't let go. You have any suggestions? I've prevented your assassination, but how the heck am I going to get out of here?' He was beginning to become really worried.

After meditating, Briskin said, 'I could ask the Chicago police . . .'

'Niddy,' Cravelli said, in derision. 'They wouldn't come.' He knew that for a certainty. 'They have no jurisdiction up here; that's been tested countless times — this isn't part of the United States, even, let alone Chicago.'

Briskin said, 'All right. I can send some party volunteers up to help you. They'll go where I say. We have a few who've clashed on the streets with Engel's organization; they might know exactly what to do.'

'That's more like it,' Cravelli said, relieved. But his stomach was still killing him; he could scarcely stand the pain and he wondered if there were any way he could obtain a glass of milk. 'The tension's getting me down,' he said. 'And I haven't had my dinner. They'll have to get up here pretty soon, or frankly I'm going to fold up. I thought of taking George Walt off the satellite entirely, but I'm afraid I'd never get them to the launch field. We'd have to pass too many Golden Door employees on the way.'

'You're directly over N'York now,' Jim Briskin said. 'So it won't take too long to get a few people there. How many do you want?'

'Certainly at least a hopper-load. Actually, all you can spare. You don't want to lose your future Attorney General, do you?'

'Not especially.' Briskin seemed calm, but his dark eyes were bright. He plucked at his great handlebar mustache, then, pondering. 'Maybe I'll come along,' he decided.

'Why?'

'To make sure you get away.'

'It's up to you,' Cravelli said. 'But I don't recommend it. Things are somewhat hot, up here. Do you know any girls at the satellite who could lead you through to George Walt's office?'

'No,' Jim Briskin said. And then a peculiar expression appeared on his face. 'Wait. I know one. She was down here in Chicago today but perhaps she's gone back up again.'

'Probably has,' Cravelli said. 'They flit back and forth like lightning bugs. Take a chance on it, anyhow. I'll see you. And watch your step.' He rang off at that point.

As he started to board the big jet-bus, which was filled with R-L volunteers, Jim Briskin found himself facing two familiar figures.

'You can't go to the satellite,' Sal Heim said, stopping him. Beside him Patricia stood somberly in her long coat, shivering in the evening wind that drew in off the lakes. 'It's too dangerous . . . I know George Walt better than you do — remember? After all, I had you figured for a business deal with them; that was to be my contribution.'

Pat said, 'If you go there, Jim, you'll never come back. I know it. Stay here with me.' She caught hold of his arm, but he tugged loose.

'I have to go,' he told her. 'My gunsel is there and I have to get him away; he's done too much for me just to leave him there.'

'I'll go instead of you,' Sal Heim said.

'Thanks.' It was a good offer, well meant. But — he had to repay Tito Cravelli for what he'd done; obviously he had to see that Tito got safely away from the Golden Door Moments of Bliss satellite. It was as simple as that. 'The best I can offer you,' he said, 'is the opportunity to ride along.' He meant it ironically.

'All right,' Sal said, nodding. 'I'll come with you.' To Pat he said, 'but you stay down below here. If we get back, we should be showing up right away — or not at all. Come on, Jim.' He climbed the steps into the jet-bus, joining the others already there.

'Take care of yourself,' Pat said to Jim Briskin.

'What did you think of my speech?' he asked her.

'I was in the tub; I only heard part of it. But I *think* it was the best you ever made. Sal said so, too, and he heard it all. Now he knows he made a terrific mistake; he should have stuck with you.'

'Too bad he didn't,' Jim said.

'You wouldn't say something along the lines of "better late than . . ."'

'Okay,' he said. 'Better late than never.' Turning, he followed Sal Heim onto the jet-bus. He had said it, but it was not true.

Too much had happened; too late was too late. He and Sal had split forever. And both of them knew it . . . or rather, feared it. And sought instinctively for a new rapprochement without having any idea how it could be done.

As the jet-bus whirled upward in brisk ascent, Sal leaned over and said, 'You've accomplished a lot since I saw you last, Jim. I want to congratulate you. And I'm not being ironic. Hardly that.'

'Thanks,' Jim Briskin said, briefly.

'But you'll never forgive me for handing you my resignation when I did, will you? Well, I can't really blame you.' Sal was silent, then.

'You could have been Secretary of State,' Jim said.

Sal nodded. 'But that's the way the fifty yarrow stalks fall. Anyhow, I hope you win, Jim. I know you will, after that speech; that certainly was a masterpiece of promising everything to everybody — a billion gold chickens in a billion gold pots. Needless to say I think you'll make a superb president. One we all can be proud of.' He grinned warmly. 'Or am I making you sick?'

The Moments of Bliss satellite lay directly ahead of them; in the center of the breast-shaped landing field the winking pink nipple guided their vehicle to its landing, a mammary invitation beckoning to all. The principle of Yin, out in space, inflated to cosmic proportions.

'It's a wonder George Walt can perambulate,' Jim said. 'Joined at the base of the skull, the way they are. Must be damned awkward.'

'What's your point?' Sal sounded tense and irritable now.

Jim Briskin said, 'No particular point. But you'd think one would have sacrificed the other long ago, for purpose of utility.'

'Have you ever actually seen them?'

'No.' He had never even been to the satellite.

'They're fond of each other,' Sal Heim said.

The jet-bus began to settle on to the landing field of the satellite; the spin of the satellite provided its constant magnetic flux, sufficient to hold smaller objects to it, and Jim Briskin thought, That's where we made our mistake. We should never have allowed this place to become attractive — in any sense whatsoever. It was feeble wit, but the best he could manage under the circumstances. Maybe Pat's right, he realized. Maybe I — and Sal Heim — will never return from this place. It was not the sort of thought he enjoyed thinking; the Golden Door satellite was not at all the kind of place he wanted to wind up. Ironic that I should be going here now, for the first time, under these circumstances, he said to himself.

The doors of the jet-bus slid back as the bus rolled to a halt.

'Here we are,' Sal Heim said, and got quickly to his feet. 'And here we go.' Along with the party volunteers he moved towards the nearest exit. Jim Briskin, after a moment, followed.

At the entrance gate the pretty, dark-haired, unclad attendant on duty smiled a white-tooth smile at them and said, 'Your tickets, please.'

'We're all new here,' Sal Heim said to her, getting out his wallet. 'We'll pay in cash.'

'Are there any girls you wish to visit in particular?' the attendant asked, as she rang the money up on her register.

Jim Briskin said, 'A girl named Sparky Rivers.'

'ALL OF YOU?' The attendant blinked, then shrugged her bare shoulders urbanely. 'All right, gentlemen. *De gustibus non disputandum est*. Gate three. Watch your step and don't jostle, please. She's in room 395.' She pointed toward gate three and the group moved in that direction.

Ahead, beyond gate three, Jim Briskin saw rows of gilded, shining doors; over some lights glowed and he understood that those were empty at the moment of customers. And, on each door, he saw the curious animated pic of the girl within; the pics called, enticed, whined at them as they approached each in turn, searching for room 395.

'Hi there!'

'Hello, big fellow.'

'Could you hurry? I'm waiting...'

'Well, how are *you*?'

Sal Heim said, 'It's down this way. But you don't need her, Jim; I can take you to their office.'

Can I trust you? Jim Briskin asked himself silently. 'All right,' he said. And hoped it was a wise choice.

'This elevator,' Sal said. 'Press the button marked C.' He entered the elevator; the rest of the group followed, crowding in after him, as many as could make it. More than half the group remained outside in the corridor. 'You follow us,' Sal instructed them. 'As soon as you can.'

Jim touched the C button and the elevator door shut soundlessly. 'I'm depressed,' he said to Sal. 'I don't know why.'

'It's this place,' Sal said. 'It isn't your style at all, Jim. Now, if you were a necktie or a flatware or a poriferous vobile salesman, you'd like it. You'd be up here every day, health permitting.'

'I don't believe so,' Jim said. 'No matter what line of work I was in.' It went against everything ethical — and esthetic — in his makeup.

The elevator door slid back.

'Here we are,' Sal said. 'This is George Walt's private office.' He spoke matter of factly. 'Hello, George Walt,' he said, and stepped out of the elevator.

The two mutants sat at their big cherrywood desk in their specially constructed wide couch. One of the bodies sagged like a limp sack and one eye had become fused-over and empty, lolling as it focussed on nothing.

In a shrill voice the head said, 'He's dying. I think he's even dead; you know he's dead.' The active eye fixed malignantly on Tito Cravelli, who stood with his laser rifle, on the far side of the office. In despair, one of the living hands poked at the dangling, inert arm of its companion body. 'Say something!' the head screeched. With immense difficulty the living body struggled to its feet; now its silent companion flopped against it and in horror it pushed the burdening lifeless sack away.

A faint spasm of life stirred the dangling sack; it was not quite dead. And, on the face of the uninjured brother, wild hope appeared. At once it tottered grotesquely toward the door.

'Run!' the head bleated, and clumsily groped for escape. 'You can make it!' it urged its still-living companion. The four-legged, scrambling joint creature bowled over the surprised volunteers at the door; together they all went down in a floundering heap, the mutant among them, squealing in panic as the injured body buried the other beneath it, struggling to rise.

Jim Briskin, as George Walt lurched upright, dived at them. He caught hold of an arm and hung on.

The arm came off.

He held onto it as George Walt stumbled up to their four feet and out the office door, into the corridor beyond.

Staring down at it, he said, 'The thing's artificial.' He handed it to Sal Heim.

'So it is,' Sal agreed, stonily. Tossing the arm aside he hastily ran after George Walt; Jim accompanied him and together they followed the mutants along the thick-carpeted corridor. The three-armed organism moved badly, crashing into itself as its twin bodies swung first wide apart and then stunningly together. It sprawled, then, and Sal Heim seized the righthand body around the waist.

The entire body came loose, arm and legs and trunk. But without the head. The other body — and single head — managed, incredibly, to get up and continue on.

George Walt was not a mutant at all. It — he — was an ordinarily-constituted individual. Jim Briskin and Sal watched him go, his two legs pumping vigorously, arms swinging.

After a long time Jim said, 'Let's — get out of here.'

'Right.' Nodding in agreement, Sal turned to the party volunteers who had trickled out into the corridor behind them. Tito Cravelli emerged from the office, rifle in hand; he saw the severed one-armed trunk which had been half of the two mutants, glanced up swiftly with perceptive understanding as the remaining portion disappeared from view past a corner of the corridor.

'We'll never catch them now,' Tito said.

'*Him*,' Sal Heim corrected bitingly. 'I wonder which one of them was synthetic, George or Walt. And why did he do it? I don't understand.'

Tito said, 'A long time ago one must have died.'

They both stared at him.

'Sure,' Tito said calmly. 'What happened here today must have happened before. They were mutants, all right, joined from birth, and then the one body perished and the surviving one quickly had this synthetic section built. It couldn't have gone on alone without the symbiotic arrangement because the brain — ' He broke off. 'You saw what it did to the surviving one just now; he suffered terribly. Imagine how it must have been the first time, when . . .'

'But he survived it,' Sal pointed out.

'Good for him,' Tito said, without irony. 'I'm frankly glad he did; he deserved to.' Kneeling down, he inspected the trunk. 'It looks to me as if this is George. I hope he can get it restored. In time.' He rose, then. 'Let's get upstairs and back to the field; I want to get out of here.' He shivered. 'And then I want a glass of warm, non-fat milk. A big one.' The three of them, with the party volunteers struggling behind, made their way silently

back to the elevator. No one stopped them. The corridor, mercifully, was empty. Without even a pic to leer and cajole at them.

When they arrived back in Chicago, Patricia Heim met them
and at once said, 'Thank God.' She put her arms around her husband, and he hugged her tight. 'What happened? It seemed to
take so long, and yet it actually wasn't long at all; you've only
been gone an hour.'

'I'll tell you later,' Sal said shortly. 'Right now I just want to
take it easy.'

'Maybe I'll cease advocating shutting the Golden Door satellite down,' Jim said suddenly.

'What?' Sal said, astonished.

'I may have been too hard. Too puritanical. I'd prefer not to
take away his livelihood; it seems to me he's earned it.' He felt
numb right now, unable really to think about it. But what had
shocked him the most, changed him, had not been the sight of
George Walt coming apart into two entities, one artificial, one
genuine. It had been Lurton Sands' disclosure about the mass of
maimed bibs.

He had been thinking about this, trying to see a way out.
Obviously, if the maimed bibs were to be awakened at all they
would have to be last in sequence. And by then perhaps replace-
ment organs would be available in supply from the UN's organ
bank. But there was another possibility, and he had come onto
it only just now. *George Walt's corporate existence proved the
workability of wholly mechanical organs.* And in this Jim Briskin
saw hope for Lurton Sands' victims. Possibly a deal could be
made with George Walt; he — or they — would be left alone if
they would reveal the manufacture of their highly sophisticated
and successful artificial components. It was, most likely, a West
German firm; the cartels were most advanced in such experi-

mentation. But it could of course be engineers under contract to the satellite alone, in permanent residence there. In any case, four hundred lives represented a great number, worth any effort at saving. Worth any deal, he decided, with George Walt which could be brought off.

'Let's get something warm to drink,' Pat said. 'I'm freezing.' She started toward the front door of Republican-Liberal party headquarters, key in hand. 'We can fix some synthetic nontoxic coffee inside.'

As they stood around the coffee pot waiting for it to heat, Tito said, 'Why not let the satellite decline naturally? As emigration begins it can serve a steadily dwindling market. You implied something along those lines in your Chicago speech anyhow.'

'I've been up there before,' Sal said, 'as you know. And it didn't kill me. Tito's been there before, too, and it didn't warp or kill him.'

'Okay, okay,' Jim said. 'If George Walt leaves me alone, I'll leave them alone. But if they keep after me, or if they won't make a deal regarding artiforg construction — then it'll be necessary to do something. In any case the welfare of those four hundred bibs comes first.'

'Coffee's ready.' Pat said, and began pouring.

Sipping, Sal Heim said, 'Tastes good.'

'Yes,' Jim Briskin agreed. In fact the cup of hot coffee, synthetic and non-toxic as it had to be (only low-stratum dormhoused Cols drank the genuine thing) was exactly what he needed. It made him feel a lot better.

Although the time was dreadfully late at night, Myra Sands had made up her mind to call Art and Rachael Chaffy at their dorm. She had reached a decision regarding their case, and the moment had arrived to tell them.

When the vidphone connection had been made to their public hall booth, Mrs Sands said, 'I'm sorry to bother you so late, Mr Chaffy.'

'That's all right,' Art said, sleepily. Obviously, he and his wife had gone to bed. 'What is it?'

'I think you should go ahead and have your baby,' Myra said.

'You do? But . . .'

'If you had listened to Jim Briskin's Chicago speech, you would know why,' Myra said. 'There'll soon be a need for new families; everything has changed. My advice to you and your wife is to apply to Terran Development for permission to emigrate by means of their new system. You might as well be among the first. You deserve to be.'

Bewildered, Art Chaffy said, 'Emigrate? You mean they finally found a place? We don't have to stay here?'

'Buy a homeopape,' Myra said patiently. 'Go out now and get it; find a vending machine, read about the speech. It'll be on the front page. And then start packing your things.' TD will have to accept you, she knew. Because of Jim Briskin's speech. They've been deprived of a choice.

'Gee, thanks, Mrs Sands,' Art Chaffy mumbled, dazed. 'I'll tell Rachael right away; I'll wake her up. And — thanks for calling.'

'Good night, Mr Chaffy,' Myra said. 'And good luck.' She hung up, then, satisfied.

Too bad, she thought, that there's no way I can celebrate. Unfortunately no one else is up this late. Because that's what this calls for: some kind of a party.

But at least she could go to bed tonight with a clear conscience.

For perhaps the first time in years.

8

FOR SEVENTY YEARS Leon Turpin had ruled the great industrial syndrome which comprised the enterprise Terran Development. A *jerry*, Turpin was now one hundred and two years old and still vigorous mentally, although physically frail. The problem for a man of his age lay in the area of the unforeseen accident; a broken hip would never mend and would put him permanently in bed.

However, no such accident had yet occurred to him, and, as was his custom, he arrived at the central administrative offices of TD, located in Washington, D.C., at eight in the morning. His chauffeur let him off at his own entrance, and from there he was raised by special lift to his floor of the building and his constellation of offices, through which he moved during the working day by three-wheeled electric cart.

Today the elderly chief of TD twitched with ill-concealed nervousness as his lift raised him to floor twenty. Last night he had heard someone, a political candidate of some sort, discussing what up to then Turpin had imagined to be his corporation's top secret. Now TD's hand was tipped. Anxiously, Leon Turpin tried to picture to himself the possible means by which the news had leaked out. Politics is the enemy of a sound economic entity, he mused. New laws, harsher tax rates, meddling . . . and now this. When, as a matter of fact, he himself had not even had an opportunity to inspect this new development.

Today he would visit the scene of the technological break-through. Possibly, if it was safe, he would pass over to the other side.

Turpin liked to see these things with his own eyes. Other-wise he could not quite grasp what was happening.

As he stepped cautiously from the lift, he made out the sight of his administrative assistant, Don Stanley, coming toward him. 'Can we go over?' he asked Don Stanley. 'Is it safe? I want to see it.' He felt eager desire rising up inside him.

Stanley, a portly man, bald with heavy-rimmed glasses, said, 'Before we do that, Mr Turpin, I'd like to show you the stellar shots they took over there.' He took hold of Leon Turpin's arm, supporting him. 'Let's sit down, sir, and discuss this.'

Disappointed, Turpin said, 'I don't want to see any charts; I want to go there.' However, he seated himself with Stanley beside him opening a large manila envelope.

'The stellar charts show,' Stanley said, 'that our initial appraisal of the situation was incorrect.'

'It's Earth,' Leon Turpin said. He felt keenly discouraged.

'Yes,' Stanley said.

'Past or future?'

Stanley, rubbing his lower lip, said, 'Neither. If you'll look at the star chart, which . . .'

'Just tell me,' Turpin said. He could not decipher the star chart; his eyes were not that good any more.

'Suppose we go over there now,' Stanley said, 'and I'll do my best to show you. It's perfectly safe; our engineers have shored up the nexus, expanded and reinforced it, and we're experimenting with the idea of a broader power supply.'

'You're really sure we'll get back?' Turpin asked querulously. 'I understand there's a girl over there who killed somebody.'

Don Stanley said, 'We've caught her. A group of company police went across; she didn't try to fight it out with them, fortunately. She's in N'York now. Held by the New York state police.' He assisted Turpin in rising to his feet. 'Now, as to the stellar chart: I feel like a Babylonian when I start talking about "celestial bodies" and their positions, but . . .' He glanced at Turpin, 'There's nothing to distinguish it from a sky-shot taken on this side of the tube.'

What that signified, Leon Turpin could not tell. However, he said, 'I see,' and nodded soberly. Eventually, he knew, his vice presidents and executive staff, including Stanley, would explain it to him.

'I'll tell you who we've got to conduct you across,' Don Stanley said. 'To be entirely on the safe side we've hired Frank Woodbine.'

Impressed, Leon Turpin said, 'Good idea. He's that famous deep-space explorer, isn't he? The one who's been to Alpha Centaurus and Proxima and . . .' He could not recall the third star-system which Woodbine had visited; his memory was just not what it once had been. 'He's an expert,' Turpin finished lamely, 'in visiting other planets.'

'You'll be in good hands,' Stanley agreed. 'And I think you'll like Woodbine. He's competent, integrated, although you never know what he's going to say. Woodbine sees the world in his own creative way.'

'I like that,' Turpin said. 'You've notified our PR people that we have Woodbine on the payroll, of course.'

'Absolutely,' Stanley said. 'There'll be teams from all the media along, catching everything you and Woodbine do and say. Don't worry, Mr Turpin; your trip across will be well-covered.'

Tickled, Leon Turpin giggled in glee. 'Terrific!' he exclaimed. 'I think you've done a good job, Don. It'll be an adventure, going over there to . . .' He broke off, again puzzled. 'Where did you say it is? It's Earth; I understand that. But . . .'

'It'll be easier to show you than to tell you,' Stanley said 'So let's wait until we're actually there.'

'Yes, of course,' Leon Turpin said. He had always found that it paid to do what Don Stanley told him; he trusted Stanley's judgment completely. And, as he aged, he trusted Don more and more.

On the second subsurface level of TD's Washington plant, Leon Turpin met the deep-space explorer Frank Woodbine, about whom he had heard so much. To his vast surprise, he found Woodbine to be dainty and slight. The man was dapper, with a tiny waxed mustache and rapidly blinking eyes. When they shook, Woodbine's hand was soft and a little damp.

'How'd you ever get to be an explorer?' Turpin asked bluntly; he was too old, too experienced, to beat around the bush.

Stammering slightly, Woodbine said, 'Bad blood.'

Turpin, amused, laughed. 'But you're good. Everybody knows that. What do you know about this place we're going to?' He had spied the Jiffi-scuttler within which the breakthrough had occurred; it was surrounded by TD researchers and engineers — and armed company guards.

'I know very little,' Woodbine said. 'I've studied the star charts that have been taken, and I don't argue the fact that it's Earth on the other side; that's certain.' Woodbine had on his heavy trouble-suit, with helmet, supply of oxygen, propulsion jets, meters and atmosphere analysis gear, and, of course, two-way com system. Always he was pictured gotten up this way; everyone expected it of him. 'It's not my job to make a decision in this matter; that's up to your company geologists.'

Puzzled, Turpin turned to Don Stanley. 'I didn't know we had any geologists.'

'Ten of them,' Stanley said.

'Your astrophysicists have done all they can,' Woodbine said. 'Now that the observation satellite has been launched.' Seeing that Turpin did not understand, he amplified. 'Earlier this morning, a Queen Bee satellite and launcher were taken through to the other side, and the satellite was successfully put into orbit; it's already sending back TV reports of what it sees.'

'That's correct,' Don Stanley added. 'So far it's functioning perfectly. From that vantage point we can learn more about this other world in an hour than fifty surface teams can learn in a year. But of course we're going to augment the TB's data with geological analysis; that's what Woodbine was referring to. And we've borrowed a botanist from Georgetown University; he's over there right now, inspecting plants. And there's a zoologist on the way from Harvard; he should arrive any time now.' After a pause, Stanley said thoughtfully, 'And we've contacted the sociology and anthropology departments at the University of Chicago to stand by in case we need them.'

'Hmm,' Turpin said. What did *that* mean, for heaven's sake? He was lost. Anyhow, Stanley and Frank Woodbine appeared to have the situation well in hand; evidently there was nothing to worry about. Even if he did not quite comprehend the situation, they did.

'I'm anxious to go over,' Woodbine said. 'I haven't been there yet, Turpin; they asked me to wait for you.'

'Then let's get started,' Turpin said eagerly. 'Lead the way.' He started toward the 'scuttler.

Frank Woodbine lit a cigar. 'Good enough. But don't be too disappointed, Turpin, if it leads us right back here. This breakthrough may be nothing but a doorway to our own world, a connection with some remote spot, say the extreme northern part of India where I understand native trees and grasses are still allowed to grow wild. Or it may turn out to be an African bird sanctuary.' He grinned. 'That will upset my good friend Mr Briskin, if it's so.'

'Briskin?' Leon Turpin echoed. 'I've heard of him. Oh yes; he's that political fellow.'

'He's the one who made the speech,' Don Stanley said, accompanying the two of them through the small mob of engineers and researchers, up to the hooped entrance of the 'scuttler.

Puffing out clouds of gray cigar smoke, Woodbine stepped through the hoop and into the tube. Assisting Leon Turpin, Stanley followed. The three of them were at once followed by a gang of TV cameramen and homeopape autonomic recording machines as well as human reporters. Already the data-gathering extensors of the media were busily at work, collecting, recording, transmitting all. Woodbine did not seem to be bothered, but Leon Turpin felt slightly irritable. Publicity was of course necessary, but why did they have to push so close? I guess they're just interested, he decided. Doing their job. Can't blame them; this is important, especially with Woodbine here. He wouldn't have come if this wasn't something big. And they know it.

Halfway down the tube of the Jiffi-scuttler Frank Woodbine conferred with a TD engineer and then stooped down. His cigar jutting stiffly ahead of him, he crept headfirst through the wall of the tube and disappeared.

'I'll be darned!' Turpin said, amazed. 'Can I get through there, Don? I mean, it's all been tested, like you said; it's safe?'

With the assistance of three TD engineers Turpin managed to kneel down and crawl tremulously after Woodbine. Felt like a kid again, Turpin said to himself, experiencing both fear and delight. Haven't done anything like this in ninety years. The wall of the tube shimmered before him. 'You in there somewhere, Frank?' he called as he gingerly made his way forward.

The shimmer passed over him, and now he saw blue sky and a horizontal procession of great trees.

Taking hold of him by the shoulders, Woodbine lifted Turpin to his feet and set him upright on the grass-covered soil. The air smelled of weird things. Leon Turpin inhaled, perplexed; the scents were old and familiar, but he could not place them. I've experienced this before, in my childhood, sometime, he said to himself. Back in the twentieth century.; Yes, this certainly is Earth; nothing else could smell this way. This is no alien, foreign planet. But was that good or bad? He did not know.

Bending, Woodbine picked a meager white flower. 'Have a morning glory,' he said to Turpin.

Ahead of them, TD space engineers sat at mobile high-frequency receiving equipment; they were no doubt accepting communications from the Queen Bee satellite somewhere overhead. The 'scope of the central van revolved slowly, a peculiar presence on this pastoral landscape.

'We're particularly interested in what it obtains from the dark side,' Don Stanley said. 'That's where it is, now.'

Glancing at him, Woodbine said, 'Lights, you mean.'

'Yes.' Stanley nodded.

'Lights of what?' Turpin asked.

'If there are lights,' Stanley said patiently, 'anywhere, in any quantity, it means that this place is inhabited by a sentient race.' He added, 'It's found roads, already, on the sun side. Or at least what appear to be roads. The QB isn't by any means the best observation satellite; actually it was selected because it's the easiest and quickest to launch. We'd follow it up in a few days with more sophisticated equipment, of course.'

'If a developed society exists here,' Woodbine said, 'it'll be of enormous importance anthropologically. But it'll hurt Jim Briskin. His whole speech took as its premise the unestablished fact that this planet is vacant and available for colonization. I don't know which to hope for; I'd personally like to see the bibs revived and conveyed here, but . . .'

'Yes,' Turpin agreed. 'We put a fortune into those language translating machines, decades ago, and never got anything back. Woodbine, *where do you think we are?*'

'You figure it out, Turpin,' Woodbine said with a spasmodic grimace. 'After all, you people built the 'scuttler. In fact, you invented it. I don't work by a priori theory; I'm a data type. I have to gather a good deal of information before I can figure out what's going on.' He gestured. 'Like those people who followed us over here.' Behind them the media reporters had appeared, still hard at work at their job of scrutinizing everything in sight. They did not appear very awed by what they had found so far.

'I don't care about the bibs,' Turpin said candidly. He saw no need to obscure his personal convictions. 'And I certainly don't care about what happens to that politician, whatever his name is. Briskett or Briskman—you know, the one who made the speech. That's not my problem; I've got other things to worry about. For instance . . .' He broke off, because a communications systems engineer was coming toward them, temporarily leaving the gear which monitored the satellite. 'Maybe this man can tell us something,' Turpin said. 'But I'll say one thing more: when I look around here all I see is grass and trees, so if it's inhabited, its tenants certainly don't have full control of the environment. That might leave room for limited colonization.'

The com-sys engineer said respectfully, 'Mr Turpin, you don't know me but I'm Bascolm Howard; I work for you and have been for years. It's a great honor for me to give you the news that the QB satellite has picked up sequences and arrangements of lights on the dark side of this body. There's absolutely no doubt about it; they're assemblages of habitation. In other words, towns.'

'Well, that's that,' Stanley said.

'Not at all,' Woodbine said sharply. To Howard he said, 'Where are these conglomerations of lights? Where they're supposed to be?'

Frowning, Howard said, 'I don't quite . . .'

'At London?' Woodbine said. 'Paris? Berlin? Warsaw? Moscow? All the big centers?'

'Some are in the right places,' Howard said. 'But some aren't. For instance, we're picking up no lights from the British Isles, and there should be colossal numbers, there. And, oddly, the image transmitted from above Africa shows many lights. Many more than there ought to be. But overall there are distinctly fewer lights than we're accustomed to; we noticed it right away. Perhaps only one third or one fourth as many as anticipated.'

'As anticipated where?' Woodbine said. 'Back home? But we're not back home, are we? Or don't you believe that? What is your operating theory? Just where do you imagine you are?'

Flushing, Howard said, 'It's not my job to figure out where I am; I was told to come here and set up monitoring systems for a QB satellite, and that's what I've done. We've had sufficient rotations already to assure us that we're on Terra; we've seen all the normal land-mass outlines, all the familiar continents and islands. Personally, I'm content simply to accept the obvious fact that this is our own world, although somehow altered; as, for example, the reformation of light-clusters. And, in addition, we've not been able to pick up transmissions from any satellite except the QB launched earlier today. The air is dead.'

'On what frequencies?' Woodbine said.

'On every frequency we've tried. Starting with the thirty-meter band and working on up.'

'Nothing?' Woodbine persisted. 'Nothing at all? That's impossible. Unless we're back before the days of radio.' He glanced at Stanley and Turpin. 'Back before 1900. But even so the U.K.

should be lit up; it's one of the most densely populated areas in the world and was such back in the 1900s . . . back for centuries. I don't understand.'

'Cloud layers?' Stanley asked Howard. 'Masking the surface?'

'Possibly,' Howard said. 'But that wouldn't explain the concentration of lights on the African Continent. Nothing explains that.'

'We must have gone ahead into the future,' Stanley said.

'Then why no radio transmissions on any frequency?' Woodbine said.

'Maybe they don't need to use the airwaves any more,' Stanley said. 'Maybe they communicate by direct mind-to-mind telepathy or something on that order which we know nothing about.'

'But the sky map,' Woodbine said. 'The stellar charts which your astrophysicists developed distinctly set the time as being identical with ours. We're coeval with this world, whether we like it — or can make up a theory about it — or not. Let's face this fact and not try to weasel around it. But why waste time theorizing? All we really have to do is make physical contact with one of these illuminated settlements and we'll know the answers.' He looked extremely impatient. 'Haul some sort of vehicle over here, a jet-hopper perhaps, and let's get started.'

Stanley said, 'There is a 'hopper over here already. From the beginning, we intended to provide Mr Turpin with an aerial view. After all, this entire place, whatever it is, belongs to him.'

Snorting, Woodbine said, 'The government may have something to say about that. Especially if Briskin is elected, which I understand is certain now.'

'We'll fight it in the courts,' Turpin said. 'Typical socialism, bureaucratic governmental interference in the free enterprise system; we've had enough of that. Anyhow, TD and TD alone has the means of getting over here. Or does the fedgov plan to seize the 'scuttler?'

'Very probably it does,' Woodbine said. 'Or will, after Briskin is in. Even Bill Schwarz may want to; he's not that stupid.'

Bristling, Turpin said, 'Look here, Woodbine, you're working for TD; now. Our opinion is your opinion, whether you like it or not. This place is company property, and no one can come here without TD's permission. And that includes you,' Turpin said, turning toward the news media people. 'So watch your step.'

'Just a moment,' Howard said. 'The boys want me back.' He hurried over to his post at the monitoring gear. Presently he returned, a perplexed expression on his face. 'They're picking up no lights from Australia,' he said. 'But a tremendous concentration from Southeast Asia and from the region of the Gobi Desert. The greatest concentrations yet. And all throughout China. But none in Japan.'

'Where are we on the planet's surface?' Woodbine asked. 'According to the QB?'

'In North America on the East Coast. Near the Potomac. Where the TD central complex is located — or at least in that vicinity, give or take ten miles.'

'There's no TD here,' Woodbine said. 'And no Washington D.C. So that's that. We haven't gone through a circular doorway and found ourselves led back to a remote area of our own world. This may be Earth, but it's obvious that it isn't *our* Earth. In that case, whose is it? And how many Earths are there?'

'I thought there was only one,' Turpin said.

'And they used to think that one was flat,' Woodbine reminded him. 'You learn as you go along. I'd like to get into that jet-hopper right now, if no one objects, and get started surveying. Is that agreeable, Turpin?'

'Yes, it is,' Turpin said eagerly. 'What do you think we'll find,

Frank? Is this more or less exciting than exploring planets in other star systems?' He chuckled knowingly. 'I can see you're all steamed up, Frank; this situation has got you hooked.'

Shrugging, Woodbine said, 'Why not?' He started toward the jet-hopper; Leon Turpin and Stanley followed. 'I never implied I was jaded; I certainly am not about to fall asleep over this.'

'I know what this is!' Leon Turpin bleated excitedly. 'Listen, this is a parallel Earth, in another universe; do you get it? Maybe there are hundreds of them, all alike physically but you know, branching off and evolving differently.'

Sourly, Woodbine said, 'Let's not go up in the 'hopper; let's just stand here in one spot with our eyes shut and theorize.'

But I know I'm right, Leon Turpin said to himself. I've got a sure instinct, sometimes; that's how I rose to be chairman of the board of directors of TD. Frank Woodbine will find out, pretty soon, and he'll have to apologize to me. I'll wait for that and not say anything more.

Together, Woodbine and Stanley assisted the old man in entering the 'hopper. The hatch slid shut; the 'hopper rose in the air and headed out across the meadow and over the nearby great trees.

If that's true, Turpin realized suddenly, then TD owns an entire Earth. And, since I control TD, what Don Stanley said is true; Earth belongs to me. This particular Earth, anyhow. But isn't one as good as another? They're all equally real.

Rubbing his hands together with excitement, Turpin said, 'Isn't this a lovely virgin place? Look at that forest down below; look at all that timber!' And mines, he realized. Maybe there's never been any coal mined here or oil wells sunk. All the metals, all the ores, may still be buried, on this particular Earth — unlike our own, where everything valuable has been brought up long ago.

I'd rather possess this one than our own, Turpin said to himself. Any day. Who wants a worn-out world, thoroughly exploited over tens of centuries?

'I'll carry it to the Supreme Court,' he said aloud, 'with the finest legal minds in the world. I'll put all the financial resources of TD into this, even if it breaks the company's back. It'll be worth it.'

Both Stanley and Woodbine glanced at him sourly.

Below them, directly ahead, lay an ocean. Evidently it was the Atlantic, Turpin decided. It *looked* like the Atlantic, at least. Gazing down at the shoreline, he saw only trees. No roads, now towns — in fact no sign of human habitation of any variety whatsoever. Like it was before the damn Pilgrims showed up here, he said to himself. But he also saw no Indians, either. Strange. Assuming he was correct, assuming this was an Earth parallel to their own, why was it so underpopulated? For instance, what had become of the racial groups which had lived in North America before the whites arrived?

Could parallel Earths differ that much and still be considered authentically parallel? Unparallel is more like it, Turpin decided.

All at once in a hoarse voice, Don Stanley said, 'Woodbine, something is following us.'

Turpin looked back, but his eyes were not good enough; he made out nothing in the bright blue mid-morning sky. Woodbine, however, seemed able to see it; he grunted, rose from the controls of the 'hopper and stood peering. By autopilot, the 'hopper continued on.

'It's losing ground,' Stanley said. 'We're leaving it behind. Want to turn around and approach it?'

'What's it seem to be?' Turpin asked apprehensively. 'We better not get too close; it may shoot us down.' He cringed from the idea of an emergency crash: he was well aware of the brittleness of his bones. Any sort of unsafe landing would end his life. And he did not want it ended, just now. This was the worst possible time.

'I'll swing back that way,' Woodbine said, returning to the controls. A moment later the 'hopper had reversed its direction.

And, at last, Turpin could perceive the other object in the sky. It was clearly not a bird; no wings flapped, and anyhow it was too large. He knew, saw with his own eyes, that it was an artificial construct, a man-made vehicle.

The vehicle was hurrying off as rapidly as possible.

Woodbine said, 'It won't be long; it's very slow. You know what it looks like? A boat, a goddam boat. It's got a hull and sails. It's a flying boat.' He laughed tautly. 'It's absurd!'

Yes, Turpin thought. It does look grotesque. It's a wonder it can stay up. And now, sure enough, the boat-shaped airborne vehicle was dipping down in increasingly narrowing spirals, its sails hanging limply. The vehicle held one single person who, they could now see, was working frantically with the controls of his craft. Was he trying to land it or keep it in the air? Turpin did not know, but in any case the vehicle was about to land – or crash.

It landed. In an open pasture, away from trees.

As the 'hopper began to descend after it, the figure within leaped from the vehicle and scampered off to disappear into the closest stand of trees.

'We frightened him,' Woodbine said, as he brought the 'hopper expertly down beside the parked, abandoned craft 'But anyhow we get to examine his ship; that ought to tell us a lot, practically everything we want to know.' Immediately he slammed the cabin hatch back and scrambled out, to drop to the ground. Without waiting for Stanley or Turpin, he sprinted toward the parked alien vehicle.

As he, too, clambered out of the 'hopper Don Stanley murmured, 'It looks like it's made out of wood.' He dropped to the ground and walked over to stand beside Woodbine.

I'd better stay here, Leon Turpin decided. Too risky for me to try to get out; I might break a leg. And anyhow it's their job to inspect this flying machine. That's what I hired them for.

'It's wood, all right,' Stanley said, his voice filtering to Leon Turpin, mixing with the rushing of wind through the nearby trees. 'And a cloth sail; I guess it's canvas.'

'But what makes it go?' Woodbine said, walking all around it. 'Is it just a glider? No power supply?'

'That was certainly a timid individual in it,' Stanley said.

'How do you think a jet-hopper would look to the innocent eye?' Woodbine said severely. 'Pretty horrible. But he had the courage to follow us for a time.' He had climbed up on the vehicle and was peering inside. 'It's laminated wood,' he said suddenly. 'Very thin layers. Looks to be extremely strong.' He banged on the hull with his fist.

Stanley, examining the rear of the craft, straightened up and said, 'It has a power supply. Looks like a turbine of some kind. Or possibly a compressor. Take a look at it.'

Together, as Leon Turpin watched, Frank Woodbine and Stanley studied the machinery which propelled the craft.

'What is it?' Turpin yelled. His voice, in the open like this, sounded feeble.

Neither man paid any attention to him. He felt agitated and peeved, and he shifted about irritably, wishing they'd come back.

'Apparently,' Woodbine said, 'the turbine or whatever it is gives it an initial thrust which launches it. Then it glides for a while. Then the operator starts up the turbine once more and it receives an additional thrust. Thrust, coast, thrust, coast and so on. Odd damn way to get from one place to another. My god, it may have to land at the end of each glide. Could that be? It doesn't seem likely.'

Stanley said, 'Like a flying squirrel.' He turned to Woodbine. 'You know what?' he said. 'The turbine is made out of wood, too.'

'It can't be,' Woodbine said. 'It'd incinerate.'

'You can scrape the paint off,' Stanley said. He had a pocket knife open and was working with it. 'I'd guess this is asbestos paint; anyhow it's heat resistant. And underneath it, more laminated wood. I wonder what the fuel is.' He left the turbine, began walking all around the craft. 'I smell oil,' he said. 'I guess it could burn oil. The late twentieth century turbines and diesel engines all burned low-grade oil, so that's not too impossible.'

'Did you notice anything peculiar about the man piloting this ship?' Woodbine said.

'No,' Stanley said. 'We were too far off. I could just barely make him out.'

Woodbine said, thoughtfully, 'He was hunched. I noticed it when he ran. He loped along decidedly bent over.'

9

LATE AT NIGHT, Tito Cravelli sat in his conapt, before a genuine fire, sipping Scotch and milk and reading over the written report which his contact at Terran Development had a little earlier in the evening submitted to him.

Softly, his tape deck played one of the cloud chamber pieces by the great mid-twentieth century composer, Harry Parch. The instrument, called by Parch 'the spoils of war,' consisted of cloud chambers, a rasper, a modernized musical saw, and artillery shell casings suspended so as to resonate, each at a different frequency. And, as a ground bass accompanying the spoils of war instrument, one of Parch's hollow bamboo marimba-like inventions tapped out an intricate rhythm. It was a piece very popular these days with the public.

But Cravelli was not listening. His attention was fixed on the report of TD's activities.

The old man, Leon Turpin himself, had crossed over via the defective Jiffi-scuttler, along with various company personnel and media people. Turpin had managed to shake the reporters off and had made a sortie by jet-hopper. Something had been found on that sortie and had been carefully brought back to TD; it was now in their labs being examined. Cravelli's contact did not know precisely what it was.

However, one fact was clear. The object brought back was an artifact. It was manmade.

Apparently Jim Briskin went off half-cocked, Cravelli said to himself. We're going to emigrate — compel the bibs to emigrate — into a region already occupied. Too bad Jim didn't think of that. Too bad I didn't think of it, for that matter.

We were fooled, it appeared, by the initial visual impression of the place. It *seemed* deserted, *seemed* susceptible to immigration.

Well, it can't be helped now, he realized. Jim made his speech; we're committed. We'll have to go on, hoping that we can still pull it off anyhow. But damn it, he thought. If only we had waited one more day!

Maybe we can kill them off, he thought. Maybe they'll catch some plague from us, die like flies.

He hated himself for having such thoughts. But there it was, clear in his mind. We need the room so badly, he realized. We've *got* to have it, no matter what. No matter how we have to go about it.

But will Jim agree? He's so damn soft-hearted.

He's got to agree, Cravelli said to himself. Or it's the end — politically, for us, and in every way for the bibs.

While he was rereading the rather meager report, his door number was all at once tapped out; someone stood at the entrance to the conapt building, wanting permission to enter and visit him. Cravelli put the report away and crossed the room to the audio-video circuit which connected his apt with the front door.

'Who is it?' he said, guardedly. As always, he was somewhat wary of nocturnal visitors.

'It's me . . . Earl,' the speaker informed him. There was no video image, however; the man was standing deliberately out of range. 'Are you alone?'

Instantly Cravelli said, 'Entirely.' He pressed the release button; fifteen stories below him the door automatically opened to admit Earl Bohegian, his contact at TD. 'You'll have to get by the doorman,' Cravelli told him. 'The key word for the building today is "potato."'

Several minutes later Bohegian, a dark, somber-looking man in his late fifties, entered the apartment. With a sigh, he seated himself facing Tito Cravelli. 'How about a beer?' Cravelli asked him. 'You look tired.'

'Fine.' Bohegian nodded. 'I am tired. I just left TD; I came directly here. We're all on emergency double-shift. Frankly, I was lucky to get away at all; I told them I had a migraine headache and had to leave. So the company guards finally let me out.'

'What's up?' Cravelli said, getting the beer from the refrigerator in the kitchen.

'The thing they hauled back here,' Carl Bohegian said. 'What I mentioned in my written report. The artifact: they've been going over it, and it's apparently the damnedest junk you ever heard of. It's a vehicle of some kind; I finally managed to find that out by hanging around in the executives' washroom, drinking "Coke," and listening to stray colloquies. It's made out of wood, but it's not primitive. It's the turbine, though, that's really throwing the engineers on Level One.' Gratefully, he accepted the beer and gulped at it. 'It works by compressing gases. I'm not an engineer — you know that — so I can't help you out on technical details. But anyhow, by compressing gases it manages to freeze a trapped chamber of water. So help me, Cravelli, the rumor going around TD is that the damn thing is run by . . .' He laughed. 'Excuse me, but it's funny. It runs by expansion of the ice. The water freezes, expands as ice, and drives a piston upward with enormous force, then the ice is melted — all this happens extremely fast — and the gases expand again, which gives another thrust to the piston, driving it back down in the cylinder again. Ice! Did you ever hear of such a source of power?

'It's funnier than steam, is it?' Cravelli said.

Laughing until tears filled his eyes, Bohegian nodded. 'Yes, a lot funnier than steam. Because it's so darn cumbersome. And so utterly ineffective. You should see it. It's incredibly complicated, especially in view of the meager thrust it ultimately manages to deliver. The vehicle coasts forward on runners, not wheels, and finally gets up into the air, but just for a very few moments. Then it glides back down. It's a kind of wooden rocketship with a sail. That's what they're building on the other side of the defective 'scuttler. That's their technology. What kind of a civilization is that?' He finished his beer, set the glass down. 'The story going around TD is that one of the better engineers got into it, cranked it up, literally, and managed to fly around the lab for fifteen or sixteen seconds, at a height of about four feet, approximately waist level.'

'Your report,' Cravelli said, once more getting it out, 'says that the stellar charts made by TD's astro-physicists prove that the planet, beyond any reasonable doubt, is Earth?'

Earl Bohegian became serious, then. 'Yes, and right here in the present. There's been no time-travel at all, not even so much as a fraction of a second. Don't ask me to explain it; *they* can't explain it, and they're supposed to know about these things. I know what the old man believes, though. According to him— and evidently he hatched this out on his own—it's an Earth that started out like ours and then split off and took a different course; at least its evolution did, its development at the level of human society. Say, ten thousand years back. Maybe even further, even as far back as the Pleistocene Period. The flowers and plants seem to be identical with ours, anyhow. And the continental configurations show no deviation from ours. All the land masses are congruent with ours, so the split-off can't be too long ago. For instance San Francisco Bay. And the Gulf of Mexico. They don't differ from ours, and I understand they formed as they are now in quasi-historical times.'

'How great is the population, do they think?'

'Not great, certainly not like ours. By the number of lights on the dark side they assume that it lies in the millions — at most. And certainly not in the billions. For instance, whole areas don't appear to be inhabited at all, at least if you accept the lights as an index.'

'Maybe there's a war on,' Cravelli said, 'and they're blacked out.'

'But as the light side moves,' Bohegian said, 'there's little indication of cities, only what appear to be roads and some sort of small, town-like structures . . . they'll know more about that in a day or so. The whole business is bizarre, to say the least. Because of the total lack of radio signals, TD is beginning to speculate that, although they have developed a turbine of sorts, they for some reason haven't run onto electricity. And the use of wood, laminated and then coated with asbestos paint; it's possible — although virtually incredible — that they don't work with metal. At least not in industry.'

'What language do they speak?'

'TD doesn't even pretend to know. They're in the process of hauling a number of linguistic decoders over from the linguistics department, so when they finally manage to nab one of the citizens over there, they'll be able to converse with him or her. That should happen any time. In fact it may already have occurred after I left TD and came here. I tell you, this is going to be the *apologia pro sua vita* of every sociologist, ethnologist, and anthropologist in the world. They're going to be migrating from here to there in droves. And I don't blame them. God knows what they'll find. Is it actually possible that a culture could develop a turbine-powered, airborne craft and not have, say, a written language? Because, according to the scuttlebutt at TD, there were no letters, signs or figures anywhere on the craft, and they certainly scrutinized it thoroughly for that.'

Half to himself, Cravelli said, 'I frankly don't care what they have and have not developed. As long as there's room on their planet for immigration. Mass immigration, in terms of millions of people.'

They each had a second beer, he and Earl Bohegian, and then Bohegian departed.

You're lucky, Jim Briskin, Cravelli thought as he shut the door after Bohegian. You took a chance when you made that speech, but evidently you're going to be able to swing it after all. Unless you balk at sharing this alter-Earth with its natives . . . or unless they happen to possess some mechanism by which they can halt us.

God, I'd like to go there, Cravelli realized. See this civilization with my own eyes. Before we smear it up, as we inevitably will. What an experience it would be! They may have developed into areas which we've never even imagined. Scientifically, philosophically, even technically, in terms of machinery and industrial techniques, sources of power, medicines — in fact in every area, from contraceptive devices to visions of God. From books and cathedrals, if any, to children's toys.

We'll probably initiate events, he reflected, by murdering a few of them, just to be on the safe side. Too bad this isn't in the hands of the government; it's damn bad luck that so far it's entirely the personal property of a private business corporation. Of course, when Jim is elected, all that will change. But Schwarz. He won't do anything; he'll just sit. And TD will be permitted to go ahead in any way it chooses.

To himself Sal Heim said: I've got to arrange a meeting between Leon Turpin, head of Terran Development, and Jim Briskin.

Jim had to be photographed over there in that new world — not just talking about it, but actually *standing* on it.

And the way to make the contact, Heim realized, is through Frank Woodbine, because Jim and Frank are old-time friends. I'll get hold of Woodbine and fix it all up, and that will be that. We'll have Jim over there and maybe Frank with him, and what a boost to our campaign that'll be. We've just got to have it, that's all.

'Get on the vidphone,' he instructed his wife Pat. 'Start them searching down Frank Woodbine; you know, the deep space explorer, the hero.'

'I know,' Pat said. She lifted the receiver and asked for information.

'A hero is a good thing to have around,' Sal said meditatively as he waited. 'It always was my hope to get Jim involved with Woodbine during this campaign. Now I think we've got the exact tie-in we want.' He felt pleased with himself; he had a good idea, and he knew it. All his professional instincts told him that he was onto something, a two-birds-with-one-stone item.

On TV he had seen the media's excursion across into the other world. Along with the rest of the nation, he had witnessed scenes of blissful trees and grass and clear sky, and he had reacted vigorously. This was it, all right. As soon as he had viewed it for himself, he had realized how profound Jim's insight had been. A new epoch in human history had begun, and his candidate had called the shots right from the start. Now, if they could just get Jim over there along with Woodbine, this one last essential act . . .

'I have him,' Pat said, breaking into his thoughts. 'Here.' She held the vidphone receiver toward him. 'He knows who you are. Because of Jim, he accepted the call.'

'Mr Woodbine,' Sal said, seating himself at the vidphone. 'It's darn nice of you to take a minute or so off from your busy schedule to hear me out. Jim Briskin would like very much to visit this other world. Can you arrange it with Turpin at TD?' He explained, then, why it was vital, just in case Woodbine was ignorant of Jim's Chicago speech. But Woodbine was not ignorant of it; he understood immediately what the situation was.

'I think,' Woodbine said thoughtfully, 'that you'd better have Jim drop by my conapt. Tonight, if possible. I want to discuss with him the material we've uncovered on the far side. Before he goes across, he should know about it. I'm sure TD won't mind; they're going to release it to the media sometime tomorrow anyhow.'

'Fine,' Sal said, immensely pleased. 'I'll have him shoot right over to your place.' He thanked Woodbine profusely and then rang off.

Now let's see if I can light the proper fire under Jim, he said to himself as he dialed. Get him to do this. What if he won't?

'Maybe I can help,' Pat said, from behind him. 'I can usually persuade Jim when it's genuinely in his interest. And this certainly is, beyond a doubt.'

'I'm glad you see it this way,' Sal said, 'because I'm very anxious about this.' He wondered what material TD had uncovered in the new world; evidently, it was important. And the way Woodbine had talked, he was obviously concerned,

Hmm, Sal thought. He felt a little worried. Just a little: the first stirrings.

Frank Woodbine answered the knock on his conapt door, and there on the threshold stood his tall and very dark friend Jim Briskin, looking gloomy as always.

'It's been a hell of a long time,' Woodbine said, ushering Jim in. 'Come over here; I want to show you right away what we've turned up on the other side.' He led Jim to the long table in the living room. 'Their compressor.' He pointed to the photograph. 'There are a hundred better ways to build a compressor than this. Why'd they choose the most cumbersome way possible? You can't call a culture primitive if it's got such artifacts in it as piston engines and gas compressors. In fact, their ability to construct a power glider alone puts them out of that class automatically. And yet, something's obviously wrong. Tomorrow, of course, we'll know what it is, but I'd like to know tonight, before we establish contact with them,'

Picking up the photo of the compressor, Jim Briskin studied it. 'The homeopapes thought you'd found something like this, when you hauled that object back. According to the rumor, you've actually . . .'

'Yes,' Woodbine said. 'The rumor's correct. Here's a pic of it.' He showed Jim the photograph of the power glider, 'It's in TD's basement. They're smart, and yet they're dumb — the people on the other side, I mean. Come on along with me tomorrow; we're going to set down exactly here.' He laid out a sequence of shots taken by the QB satellite. 'Recognize the terrain? It's the coast of France. Over here . . .' He pointed. '. . . Normandy. A town of theirs. You can't call it a city, because it's simply not that large. But it's the largest one the QB has been able to detect. So we're going there to confront them in their own bailiwick. By doing so, we get a direct confrontation vis-à-vis their culture, the totality of what they've managed to develop. TD is supplying linguistics machines; we've got anthropologists, sociologists . . .' He broke off. 'Why are you looking at me like that, Jim?'

Jim Briskin said, 'I thought it was a planet in another star system. Then the hints in the media were right, after all. But I'll come with you; I'm glad to. Thanks for letting me.'

'Don't take it so hard,' Woodbine said.

'But it's inhabited,' Jim said.

'Not entirely. My god, look on the bright side. This is a tremendous event, an encounter with another civilization entirely, what I've been searching for over three star-systems and a time-period of four decades. You're not going to begrudge us that, are you?'

After a pause Jim said, 'You're right, of course. I'm just having trouble adjusting to this. Give me a little time.'

'Are you sorry now that you made that Chicago speech?'

'No,' Jim said.

'I hope your attitude doesn't have to change. There's one more thing we found: no one at TD has so far been able to make out what it signifies. Look at this pic.' He placed the glossy print before Jim. 'It was in the glider, poked down out of sight, obviously deliberately concealed. In a little leather bag.'

'Rocks?' Jim said, scrutinizing the pic.

'Diamonds. Rough, not cut. Just as they come out of the ground. The inference is that these people prize precious stones but don't know how to cut or polish them. So, in this one respect at least, they're some four or five thousand years behind us. What would you say about a culture that can build a power glider, including piston engine and compressor, but hasn't learned to cut and polish gems?'

Jim said, 'I — don't know.'

'We're taking some cut stones with us tomorrow. Couple of diamonds, opals, a gold ring set with a nice fat ruby donated by the wife of one of TD's vice presidents. And we're also taking this.' He tossed a sheet of rolled-up paper before Jim. 'A schematic of a very simple, efficient turbine. And this.' He bounced another tube of paper onto the table. 'A schematic of a medium-size steam engine, circa 1880, used as a donkey engine in mine work. But, of course, our main effort will be directed toward ferrying a few of their technological experts, if there are any, over here. Turpin wants to show them around TD, for example. And after that, probably N'York City.'

'Has the government made an effort to get involved in this?'

'Schwarz, I understand, has asked Turpin if a mixed bag of

specialists from various bureaus can accompany us tomorrow. I don't know what the old man has decided; it's up to him. After all, TD can shut down the nexus any time it so desires. Schwarz knows that.'

Jim said, 'Would you hazard any kind of estimate as to the level of their culture in terms of chronology relative to ours?'

'Sure,' Frank Woodbine said. 'Somewhere between 3000 B.C. and A.D. 1920. Does that answer your question?'

'So it can't be graded on a time-scale which compares it to us.'

'We'll know tomorrow,' Frank said. 'Or rather — and I fully expect this, Jim — we'll know that they're so damn different from us that they might as well live on a planet in some other star system, as you'd like them to be. A non-terrestrial race entirely.'

'With six legs and an exoskeleton,' Jim murmured.

'If not worse. Something that would make George Walt look perfectly ordinary. You know, that's what we ought to do: take George Walt over with us tomorrow. Tell these people on the other side that George Walt is our god, that we worship him and they'd better, too, or he'll make the bad atoms rain down on them and cause them to die of leukemia.'

'Probably,' Jim said, 'they've not reached the level of developing atomic power. Either for industry or warfare.'

'For all I know,' Frank said quietly, 'they've got an atomic tactical bomb made out of wood.'

'That's impossible. It's a joke. You're kidding.'

'I'm not kidding — I'm just terribly upset. Nobody in our world ever knew that you could build complex modern machinery out of wood, as these people have. If they can manage to do that, although God knows how long it took them to do it, they can do anything. At least, that's the way it strikes me. I'm going to set the jet-hopper down in Normandy tomorrow with my heart in my mouth, and I've been to more star-systems than any other human being; don't forget that. I've seen a lot of alien worlds.'

Somberly, Jim Briskin picked up the photo of the wooden engine and once more studied it.

'Of course,' Frank added, 'I keep saying to myself, "Look what we can learn." And look what they can learn from *us*.'

'Yes,' Jim agreed, 'we have to look on this as an opportunity.' His tone, however, was grave.

'You know, just as I know, *that something is awfully wrong*.'

Jim Briskin nodded.

In the middle of the night Don Stanley, administrative assistant to Leon Turpin, was awakened by the ringing of his vidphone.

Sitting up groggily, he managed to locate the receiver in the dark. 'Yes?' he said, switching on the light. In the bed, his wife slept on.

On the vidscreen the physiognomy of a top-level TD researcher came into view. 'Mr Stanley, we're calling you instead of Mr Turpin. Somebody at policy *has* to know this.' The researcher's voice was jumpy with tension. 'The QB is down.'

'Down what?' Stanley could not focus his faculties.

'They shot it down. God knows how. Just now, not ten minutes ago. We don't know whether we should try to put up another one to replace it or just wait.'

Stanley said, 'Maybe the QB merely malfunctioned. Maybe it's up there coasting around dead.'

'It's not up there at all; we've got a number of instruments capable of registering that. You know, bringing down an orbiting satellite requires a pretty exact science of weapons development; it's not easy to do.'

Still half-asleep, Don Stanley had a momentary hypnogogic

vision of an enormous crossbow with a cord capable of being stretched back a mile. He shook the vision off and said, 'Maybe we shouldn't send Woodbine over there tomorrow. We don't want to lose him.'

'Whatever you and Mr Turpin decide,' the researcher said. 'But sooner or later we have to make formal contact with them, don't we? So why not right away? It seems to me that, in view of their maneuver against the QB, we can't afford to wait. We've *got* to know what they possess.'

'We'll go ahead,' Stanley decided, 'but we'll see that Woodbine is accompanied by company police. And we'll keep in constant radio contact with him all the time he's there.'

'"Company police,"' the researcher said in disgust. 'What Woodbine needs is the United States Army.'

'We don't want the government meddling into this,' Stanley said sharply. 'If TD can't handle this, we'll shut down the 'scuttler and abolish the nexus. Forget the entire matter.' He felt irritable. This puts an entirely new light on everything, this about the QB, he realized. In no way — or at least in no important way — are these people lagging behind us. We're not going to be able to get away with trading them a basketful of glass beads in exchange for North America. He recalled the leather bag of uncut diamonds found in the glider. They may not be able to finish up stones, he thought, but at least they know what's really valuable. There's a crucial difference between carrying around a bagful of rough diamonds and, say, a bagful of seashells.

'You've still got a team on the other side, don't you?' Stanley said. 'You didn't pull them back over here.'

'They're there,' the researcher said, 'but they're just standing by, waiting for dawn and the party of university professors and the linguistics machines, all that stuff that's been promised.'

'We don't want to get into a brawl with these people,' Stanley said, 'even if they did get to our satellite. TD wants industrial techniques from them, wants their know-how hardwarewise. Let's not spoil that. Okay?'

'Okay,' the researcher agreed, 'and lots of luck.'

Don Stanley hung up, sat for a time, then rose and walked to the kitchen of his conapt to fix himself something to eat.

Tomorrow's going to be quite a day, he said to himself. I wish I was going along, but, in view of this, I think I'll stay on this side. After all, I'm a desk man, not a leg man; let somebody else do it. Somebody like Woodbine who's paid to take risks. This is exactly why we hired him.

He did not envy Woodbine.

And then all at once it occurred to him that old Leon Turpin might order him to go along. In which case he would have to — or lose his job. And losing one's job, these days, was no joke.

His appetite was gone. Leaving the kitchen, Don Stanley returned to his bed, gloomily aware that with such thoughts on his mind he would probably be unable to get back to sleep.

It turned out that he was right.

10

BECAUSE THE DEFECTIVE Jiffi-scuttler technically belonged to him, Darius Pethel could not effectively be denied permission to cross over, along with the group of top scientific and linguistic experts leaving in the morning. Wearing a carefully ironed and starched white shirt and new tie, he arrived at TD's central administrative offices in Washington, D.C., at exactly eight A.M. He felt confident. TD employees had treated him with deference ever since he had turned the defective 'scuttler over to them. After all, he could take it back . . . or, at least, so Pethel reasoned.

Two officials of the company, both of them tense, accompanied him to Mr Turpin's office on the twentieth floor, depositing him there, and at once hurrying off. Now he was on his own.

The board chairman of TD did not awe Darius Pethel. 'Morning, Mr Turpin,' he said in greeting. 'I hope I'm not late.' He was not sure where the group was assembling. Probably down in the subsurface labs near the 'scuttler.

'Ump,' the old man said, glancing at him sideways, the wrinkled neck twisting like a turkey's. 'Oh, yes. Pedal.'

'Pethel.'

'So you want to be in on things, do you?' Leon Turpin studied him, smiling a thin, gleeful smile.

'I want to keep in touch,' Pethel said. He pointed out, 'After all, it is my property.'

'Oh, yes, we're very conscious of that, Pethel. You're a highly important figure in all that's going on. Being a businessman, you'll no doubt be useful on this mission; you can establish trade relations with these people. In fact, we expect you to start selling them 'scuttlers.' Leon Turpin laughed. 'All right, Mr Pethel. You go ahead downstairs to the labs and join the group; make yourself at home here at TD. Do whatever you feel like. I myself — I'm staying here. One trip across is enough for a man of my age; I'm sure you can appreciate that.'

Conscious that he had been made fun of, Darius Pethel left Mr Turpin's office and took the elevator down. Smouldering, he said to himself, *I can be important in this.* The people on this alternative Earth or whatever it is can probably use an improved method of transportation even better than we can. After all, from what the TV newsman said, they seem to be backward, compared to us. There was something about a primitive ship or airplane. Something obsolete in our world several centuries ago.

The elevator let him off at the guarded lower floors of the building, and he made his way down the corridor, following the instructions painted on the walls, to the main lab proper.

When he opened the lab door he found himself facing a man whom he had seen many times on TV. It was the Republican-Liberal candidate for president, James Briskin, and Pethel halted in awe and surprise.

'Let's get a shot of you standing at the entrance hoop,' a photographer was saying to Briskin. 'Could you move over there, please?'

Obligingly, Briskin walked to the 'scuttler.

This is the big time, Pethel realized. Our next president is here along with me. I wonder what would happen if I said hello to him, he wondered. Would he answer back? Probably would because he's campaigning; after he gets into office, he won't have to.

To Jim Briskin, Pethel said humbly, 'Hello, Mr Briskin. You don't know me, but I'm going to vote for you.' He had just made up his mind; seeing Briskin in real life had decided him. 'I'm Darius Pethel.'

Glancing at him, Briskin said, 'Hello, Mr Pethel.'

'This Jiffi-scuttler belongs to me,' Pethel explained. 'I discovered the rent in it, the doorway to the other universe. Or rather, my repairman Rick Erickson did. But he's dead now.' He added, 'Very tragic; I was there when it happened.'

A TD official, appearing beside Jim Briskin, said, 'We're ready to get started, Mr Briskin.'

A small, rather handsome man strolled up, and Darius, with a start, recognized him, too. This was Frank Woodbine, the famous deep-space explorer. Good lord, Pethel said to himself, and I'm going with them!

'Jim,' Woodbine said to Jim Briskin, 'we're all carrying laser pistols except you. Don't you think you're making a mistake?'

'Hey,' Pethel said tremulously, 'nobody gave *me* a pistol.'

A TD employee passed a pistol, in its holster, over to him. 'Sorry, Mr Pethel.'

'That's more like it,' Dar Pethel said, wondering if he was supposed to hold the thing in his hands or strap it on somehow.

'I don't need a gun,' Jim Briskin said.

'Of course you do,' Woodbine said. 'You want to come back, don't you?' To Pethel, Woodbine said, 'Tell him he needs a gun.'

'You ought to have one, Mr Briskin,' Pethel said eagerly. 'No one knows what we'll run into over there.'

At last, with massive reluctance, Briskin accepted a gun. 'This is not the way,' he said, to no one in particular. 'We shouldn't be doing this, going to meet them armed like this.' He looked melancholy.

'What choice have we got?' Woodbine said and disappeared through the entrance hoop of the Jiffi-scuttler.

'I'll go in with you, Mr Briskin,' Pethel said. 'Instead of with those scientists.' He indicated the group which had formed behind them. 'I can't talk their language; I've got nothing in common with them.'

A man whom he recognized as Briskin's campaign manger, Salisbury Heim, hurried up to join Briskin. 'Sorry I'm late.' Quickly, he made note of the news photographers, TV cameras, the gang of media people. 'You fellows get every step of this,' he called to them. 'You understand?'

'Yes, Mr Heim,' they murmured, moving forward.

'The time is now,' Salisbury Heim said, and gave Jim Briskin a small push in the direction of the entrance hoop. 'Let's go, Jim.'

'Are you ready, Mr Pethel?' Jim Briskin asked.

'Oh, thanks; I am, yes,' Pethel answered hurriedly. 'This is certainly a fascinating journey, isn't it?'

'Momentous,' Salisbury Heim said.

'In fact even historical,' Briskin said, with a faint smile.

'Entering the Jiffi-scuttler now,' a TV newsman was saying into his lapel mike, 'the possible future president of the United States reveals no indication of concern for his personal safety. Solicitous of the welfare of the others surrounding him, he makes certain that they understand the gravity or — as James Briskin himself just now put it — the historical significance of this body of persons passing across into a situation fraught with possible peril. But the stakes in this are vast, and no one has forgotten that, least of all James Briskin. Another world, another civilization . . . what will this come to mean in future centuries to mankind? Undoubtedly, James Briskin is asking himself that at this very instant as he crosses the threshold of the rather plain, almost ordinary-appearing Jiffi-scuttler.'

Jim Briskin winked at Darius Pethel.

Startled, Pethel attempted to wink back, but he was too tense.

'Hey, just a moment, Mr Briskin!' a homeopape photographer called. 'We want to be sure we catch you going through the rent. Could you kindly retrace your steps back to the hoop, please? Those last four steps?'

Obligingly, Jim Briskin did so.

The TV newsman was saying, 'So now in only a matter of seconds presidential candidate James Briskin will be passing through the connecting link into a universe whose very existence was not even suspected two days ago. Authorities seem pretty well to agree now, on the basis of stellar charts taken by the no longer functioning Queen Bee satellite . . .'

I wonder why it's no longer functioning, Pethel mused. Has something gotten fouled up, over there? It didn't sound like a good omen; it made him uncomfortable.

On the other side, amid a meadow of excellently green grass and small white flowers, they, now a party of thirty, boarded *an* express jet-hopper which TD engineers had somehow managed to disassemble, pass through the rent, and then reassemble. Almost at once the 'hopper rose and soared out over the Atlantic, toward the northern coast of France.

Watching a flight of gulls, Jim Briskin thought: From this vantage point, it appears no different from our own world. The gulls disappeared behind them as the jet-hopper hurried on. Will we see ships of any sort on this ocean? he wondered.

Fifteen minutes later, by his wristwatch, he saw a ship below.

It did not seem to be large. But it was ocean-going, and that, he decided, was something. Of course it was wooden; he took that for granted, as did the others in the 'hopper, all of whom were pressed against the windows, peering out. The ship, did not have sails, but it also lacked a stack. What propels it? he wondered. More nonsense machinery. If not the expansion of ice, then by all means the popping of paper bags.

The pilot of the jet-hopper swooped low over the ship; they were treated to a thorough look, at least momentarily. Figures on the deck scampered about in agitation, then disappeared down below, lost from sight. The ship continued on. And, presently, the 'hopper left it behind.

'We didn't learn much,' Dillingsworth, the anthropologist, said in disappointment. 'How long before we reach Normandy?'

'Another half hour.' the pilot said.

They saw, then, a collection of small boats, perhaps a fishing fleet; the boats were anchored, and they did have sails. Aboard, the sailors gaped up at the sight of the 'hopper, frozen in their positions as if carved there. Again the 'hopper dipped low.

The anthropologist, staring down, said, 'Lower.'

'Can't,' the pilot answered. 'Too dangerous; we're overloaded.'

'What's the matter?' the sociologist from the University of California, Edward Marshak, asked Dillingsworth. 'What did you see?'

After a time Dillingsworth said, 'As soon as we reach the European landmass, as soon as we can land, let's do so. Let's not wait to seek out their centers of concentration; I want to have us set down by the first one of them we spot.'

The fishing boats disappeared behind them.

With shaking hands, Dillingsworth opened a textbook which he had brought, began turning pages. He did not allow anyone else to see its title; he sat off by himself in a corner of the 'hopper, a brooding, dark expression on his face.

Stanley, the senior official from TD, said inquiringly, 'Do you think we should turn back?'

'Hell no,' Dillingsworth rasped. And that was all he said; he did not amplify.

Next to Jim Briskin, the round, heavy-set little businessman from Kansas City leaned over and said, 'He makes me nervous; he's found something and he won't say what it is. It was when he saw those fishermen. I was watching his face, and he almost fainted.'

Amused, Jim said, 'Take it easy, Mr Pethel. We still have a long way to go.'

'I'm going to find out what it was,' Pethel said. He scrambled to his feet and made his way over to Dillingsworth. 'Tell me,' he said. 'Why keep it quiet? It must have been pretty bad to make you clam up like this. What could you possibly have seen in those few seconds that would make you react this way? Personally, I don't think we should go on until ...'

'Look at it this way,' Dillingsworth said. 'If I'm wrong, it doesn't matter. If I'm right ...' He looked past Pethel to Jim Briskin. 'We'll know all about it before we make our return trip, later today.'

After a pause, Jim said, 'That's good enough. For me, at least.'

Fuming, Darius Pethel returned to his seat. 'If I had known it'd be like this ...'

'Wouldn't you have come?' Jim asked him.

'I don't know. Possibly not.'

Stirring restlessly, Sal Heim said, 'I didn't realize there was going to be any hazard involved in this.'

'What did you think,' one of the newsmen asked him, 'when they took our QB satellite out?'

'I just learned about that,' Sal snapped back, 'as we were entering the damn 'scuttler.'

A photographer for one of the big homeopapes said, 'How

about a game of draw? Jacks or better to open, penny a chip but no table limit.'

Within a minute, the game had started.

Ahead, on the horizon, Sal Heim thought he saw something and he took a quick look at his wristwatch. That's Normandy, he realized. We're almost there. He felt his breath stifle in his throat; he could hardly breathe. God, I'm tense, he decided. That anthropologist really shook me. But too late to turn back now. We're fully committed; and anyhow it would look bad, politically-speaking, if Jim Briskin backed out. No, for our own good we have to continue whether we want to or not.

'Set us right down,' Dillingsworth instructed the pilot in a clipped, urgent tone of voice.

'Do so,' Don Stanley of TD chimed in. The pilot nodded.

They were over open countryside, now; the coastline had already fallen behind them, the wave-washed shore. Sal Heim saw a road. It was not much of a road, but it could hardly be mistaken for anything else, and, looking along it, he made out in the distance a vehicle, a sort of cart. Somebody going uneventfully along the road, on his routine business, Sal realized. He could see the wheels of the cart, now, and its load. And, in the front, the driver, who wore a blue cap. The driver did not look up. Evidently he was not aware of the 'hopper. And then Sal Heim realized that the pilot had cut the jets. The 'hopper was coasting silently down.

'I'm going to place it on the road,' the pilot explained. 'Directly in front of his cart.' He snapped on a retrojet, briefly, to brake the 'hopper's fall.

Dillingsworth said, 'Christ, I was right.'

As the 'hopper struck, almost all of them were already on their feet, peering at the cart ahead, trying to discover what it was that the anthropologist saw. The cart had stopped. The driver stood up in his seat and stared at the jet-hopper, at them inside it.

Sal Heim thought, There's something wrong with that man. He's — deformed.

A homeopape reporter said gruffly, 'Must be from wartime radiation, from fallout. God, he looks awful.'

'No,' Dillingsworth said. 'That's not from fallout. Haven't you seen that before? Where have you seen it before? *Think*.'

'In a book,' the little businessman from Kansas City said. 'It's in the book you have there.' He pointed at Dillingsworth. 'You looked it up after we passed those fishing boats!' His voice rose squeakily.

Jim Briskin said, 'He's one of the races of pre-humans.'

'He's of the Paleoanthropic wing of primate evolution,' Dillingsworth said. 'I'd guess Sinanthropus, a rather high form of Pithecanthropi, or Peking man, as he is called. Notice the low vault of the skull, the very heavy brow ridge which runs unbroken across the forehead above the eyes. The chin is undeveloped. These are simian features, lost by the true line of Homo sapiens. The brain capacity, however, is reasonably large, almost as great as our own. Needless to say, the teeth are quite different from our own.' He added, 'In our world, this branch of primate evolution came to an end in the Lower Pleistocene, about a million and a half years ago.'

'Have we . . . gone back in time?' the Kansas City businessman asked.

'No,' Dillingsworth said irritably. 'Not one week. Evidently here Homo sapiens either did not appear at all or for some reason did not win out. And Sinanthropus became the dominant species. As in our world we are.'

Frank Woodbine said, 'Yes, I thought he stooped. That one who jumped out of the glider yesterday.' His voice shook.

'True,' Dillingsworth agreed. 'Sinanthropus was not fully

erect. That was an advantage in plains areas where short grass grew; an erect posture would have made him a better target.' He spoke flatly. Methodically.

'God,' Sal Heim said. 'So what do we do *now?*'

There was no answer. From any of them.

What a mess, Sal Heim said to himself as the thirty of them clambered from the parked 'hopper and surrounded the stalled cart. Too frightened to try to escape, the driver continued to stare meekly at them all, clutching some sort of parcel in his arms. He wore, Sal noted, a toga-like one-piece garment. And his hair, unlike the reconstructions in the museums of dawn men, had been cut short and tidily. What repercussions there're going to be from this, Sal realized. Damn it, what rotten luck!

But it was even worse than that. Far, far worse. So Jim Briskin got beaten at the polls because of this . . . so what? That was a mere pebble in the bottom of the barrel. In an intuitive flash of insight, he saw the entire thing, spread out into their lives, ahead. His and Jim's and everyone else's . . . whites and cols alike. Because, in terms of race relations, this was an absolute calamity.

By the cart, several TD employees and Dillingsworth were rapidly setting up a linguistics machine. They evidently were going to make the attempt to communicate with the driver.

Hypnotized by the sight of the apparition seated in the cart, the little round businessman from Kansas City said stammeringly to Sal, 'Isn't it something? Given a chance these near-humans actually figured out how to lay roads and build carts. And they even made a gas turbine, the TV said.' He looked stunned.

'They had a million and a half years to do it.' Sal pointed out.

'But it's still amazing. They built that ship we saw; it was crossing the Atlantic! I'll bet there isn't an anthropologist in the world who would have made book on that — bet they could create such an advanced culture, like they have. I take off my hat to them; I think it's great. It's . . . very encouraging, don't you think? It sort of makes you realize that . . .' He struggled to express himself. '. . . that if anything happened to us, to Homo sapiens, other life forms would go on.'

It did not encourage Sal Heim.

The best thing to do, he said to himself bleakly, is to go back to our world and then plug up that goddam hole. That entrance between our universe and this. Forget it ever existed, that we ever saw this.

But we can't, because there'll always be some curious, scientific-type busybody who'll insist on poking around here. And TD itself; it'll still want to go over all the artifacts in this world to see what it can make use of. So it's just not that simple. We can't just shut our eyes, walk off, pretend it never happened.

'I don't think what these near-men have done here is so great,' Sal said aloud. 'They're pitifully backward, compared to us, and they've had ten times as long to do it in. At least ten times; maybe twenty. They haven't discovered metal, for instance. Take that one example.'

Nobody paid any attention to him. They were all gathering around the linguistics machine, waiting to see how the attempt at communication was going to go.

'So who wants to talk to that semi-ape?' Sal said bitterly. 'Who needs it?' He walked about in an aimless, futile circle. I've got to get my candidate out of here, he knew. I can't let him get identified with this.

But Jim Briskin showed no signs of leaving. In fact he had gone up to the cart and was saying something to the Peking man, talking directly to him. Probably trying to calm him down. That would be just like Jim.

You damn fool, Sal thought. You're ruining your political career; can't you see that? The ramifications of this—am I the only one who can perceive them? It ought to be obvious. But evidently it was not.

Into the microphone of the TD linguistics machine, Dillingsworth was saying over and over again, 'We're friends, We're peaceful.' To Stanley he said, 'Is this thing working or not? . . . We're friends. We come to your world in peace. We will hurt no one.'

'It takes time,' Stanley explained. 'Keep at it. See, what it has to do is take the visual images connected to the intrinsically meaningless words, images which flash up in your brain as you speak, and transmit replicas of those visual images directly to the brain of . . .'

'I know how it works,' Dillingsworth said brusquely. 'I'm just anxious for it to get started before he bolts. You can see he's getting ready to.' Into the microphone he once again said, 'We're friends. We come in peace.'

All at once the Peking man spoke.

From the audio section of the linguistics machine, a strangled noise sounded; recorded automatically, it was immediately repeated as the tape-deck rewound and played it back.

'What'd he say?' the little businessman from Kansas City demanded, looking around at everyone. 'What'd he *say?*'

Dillingsworth said into the mike, 'Are you our friend, too? Are you friends with us as we are with you?'

Going over to Jim Briskin, Sal put his hand on his shoulder and said 'Jim, I want to talk to you.'

'For God's sake, later,' Jim answered.

'Now,' Sal said. 'It can't wait.'

Jim groaned. 'Jesus, man, are you out of your head?'

'No I'm not,' Sal said evenly. 'It's everyone else here who is. Including you. Come on.' He took hold of Jim by the shoulder and propelled him forcibly from the group, off to one side of the road. 'Listen,' Sal said. 'How do you define man? Go on, define man for me.'

Staring at him Jim said. 'What?'

'Define man! I'll do it, then. Man's a tool-making animal. Okay, what's all this — for example, that cart and that hat and that package and that robe? Plus the ship we saw and that glider with that compressor and turbine? Tools. All of them, broadly speaking. So what does that make that damn creature sitting up there at the tiller of that cart? I'll tell you: it makes him a man, that's what. So he's ugly-looking; so he has a low forehead and beetling brows and he isn't too bright. But he's bright enough to get in under the wire and qualify, that's how bright he is goddam it. I mean, my god, he's even built roads. And . . .' Sal vibrated with rage. '. . . he even shot down our QB satellite!'

'Look,' Jim began, wearily, 'this is no time . . .'

'*It's the only time.* We have to get out of here. Back across and forget what we saw.' But, of course, as Sal well knew, it was hopeless. The 'hopper, for instance, belonged to TD, was piloted by a TD employee to whom Sal Heim could give no orders. Only Stanley could, and obviously Stanley had no intention of leaving; he was standing by the linguistics machine, fascinated. 'Let me ask you this,' Sal panted. 'If they're men, and you admit they are, how're we going to deny them the vote?'

After a pause Jim said, 'Is that actually what you're worrying about?'

'Yes,' Sal said.

Turning, Jim walked back to join the group. Without a word. Sal Heim watched him go.

'He's going to be voting,' Sal said, aloud but to himself. 'I can see it coming. And then you know what? Mixed marriages. Between us and them. Let's go home; please, let's go home. Okay?' No one stirred. 'I don't want to foresee it, but I do,' Sal said. 'Can

I help that? So I'm a prophet. Hell, don't blame me; blame that thing sitting up there on that cart. It's his fault. He shouldn't even be existing.'

From the audio curcuit of the linguistics machine a guttural, hoarse voice whispered, '. . . friend.'

Frantically, Dillingsworth turned to those around him and said, 'It was him; that was *not* feedback from what I put in.'

'They don't even have radio, here,' Sal Heim said.

In his N'York office, the private investigator Tito Cravelli received a puzzling bulletin from his contact at TD, Earl Bohegian: 'First report from 'hopper to TD. World inhabited by apes.'

Taking a calculated risk, Cravelli dialed Terran Development through regular vidphone channels. When he reached TD's switchboard, he matter of factly asked to speak to Mr Bohegian.

'How could you be so foolish as to call me direct?' Bohegian asked nervously, when the call was put through to his office.

'Explain your message,' Tito said.

'They're educated apes,' Bohegian said, leaning close to the vidscreen and speaking in a low, urgent voice. 'You know, missing links.'

'Dawn men,' Tito said, finally understanding. He felt his heart skip a beat. 'Go on, Earl, I want to hear it all; keep talking and if you ring off, I'll call you right back, so help me God.'

Earl Bohegian muttered, 'The report was given to old Leon Turpin; he's examining it right now on floor twenty. They're trying to decide if they want to shut the 'scuttler down and wall the rent up or not. But I don't think they're gonna, not from what I've heard.'

'No,' Tito agreed. 'They won't. There's too much to gain by leaving it open.'

'But they are sort of upset. Who isn't? Imagine; here we took it for granted that humans like ourselves . . .'

'Did the 'hopper specifically state which variety of sub-Homo sapiens it is?' Cravelli asked, trying to remember his college anthropology.

'Peking man. Does that sound right?'

Cravelli bit his lip. 'That's a hell of a low-grade type. One of the lowest. Now, if it had been Cro-Magnon or even Neanderthal. . . .' That would be another matter. After all, the Palestine archeological discoveries were proof that Homo sapiens and Neanderthal had already interbred, tens of thousands of years in the past. And it had evidently done no harm; the Homo sapiens genetic strain had dominated.

'They're going to bring one back,' Bohegian said. 'They've already got one inside the 'hopper, the scuttlebutt says down in the washroom at the end of my hall. And they're in lin-com with it. It's docile, one exec told me just now. Scared out of its wits.'

'Of course it would be,' Cravelli said. 'They probably remember us from their past, remember getting rid of us.' Just as we got rid of them in our world, he thought. Wiped them utterly out. 'And now we're back,' he said. 'It must seem like black magic to them: ghosts from a hundred thousand years ago, from their own Stone Age. Jeez, what a situation!'

'I've got to ring off,' Bohegian said. 'I told you everything anyhow, Tito. When there's more . . .'

'Okay,' Tito Cravelli said and broke the connection.

I wonder if they'll be able to pilot that jet-hopper back across the Atlantic and then back through the rent to our world, he conjectured. Or will the Peking people get them along the way? Good question.

This is going to work havoc with the November election, he

said to himself, broodingly. Who could have possibly anticipated something like this? Once more Tito Cravelli saw his Attorney Generalship receding, along with Jim Briskin's election.

These parallel worlds are a knotty problem, he realized. I
wonder how many exist. Dozens? With a different human sub-
species dominant on each? Weird idea. He shivered. God, how
unpleasant . . . like concentric rings of hell, each with its own
particular brand of torment.

And then he thought suddenly: Maybe there's one in which a
human type superior to us, one we know nothing about, domi-
nates; one which, in our own world, we extinguished at its inception. Blotto, right off the bat.

Somebody ought to tinker with a 'scuttler with that in mind,
Tito decided. But then, it occurred to him, they'd show up here,
just the way we're appearing in Peking man's orderly little universe. And we'd be finished. We wouldn't be able to survive the
competition.

Just, he thought, as Peking man isn't going to be able to stand
up to us for long.

The poor clucks. They don't know what's in store for them;
their time is limited, now. Because their ancestral foe has re-
appeared — and right in their midst, with TV, rocketships, laser
rifles, H-bombs, all kinds of devices inconceivable to their limited mentalities. They spent a million or two years developing a
gas compressor, and what good is it going to do them, now that
the chips are down? Them and their wooden gliders that travel
a hundred feet and then have to land again. My god, we've got
ships in three star systems!

And then he remembered the QB satellite.

How'd they do that? he asked himself. Remarkable! It doesn't
quite fit in. Because even so, they are an entire evolutionary step
below us.

We can lick them with both hands and one frontal lobe of our brain tied behind our backs . . . so to speak.

But the assurance of a moment ago had left him and he did not right now feel quite so secure.

Jim Briskin, he said to himself, you just better darn well get back intact from that alternate Earth. Because there's going to be a hard row to hoe, here, for all of us, and we need someone capable. I can see Bill The Cat's Meatman Schwarz attempting to deal with this problem . . . yes, how I can see it.

Once more he dialed TD's Washington, D.C., number and again, when he had their switchboard, asked for Earl Bohegian in 603.

'I want you to let me know,' Tito Cravelli instructed Bohegian when he had him, 'the moment Jim Briskin crosses back. I don't give a damn about the others — just him. Got it, Earl?'

'Sure, Tito,' Bohegian said, nodding.

'Can you get a message to him? After all, he'll be there in your building, on the bottom floor.'

'I can try,' Bohegian said, sounding dubious.

'Tell him to call me.'

'Okay,' Bohegian said dutifully, 'I'll do my best.'

Ringing off, Cravelli sat back in his chair, then searched about for a cigarette. He had done all he could — for now. Here on out he could only sit and wait, at least until Jim showed up. And, he knew, that might be a long time.

He thought, then, of something interesting. Perhaps he now understood why Cally Vale had shot and killed the 'scuttler repairman with her laser pistol. If she had run across one of the Peking men, she probably had gone straight into hysterical shock. Had probably in her state taken the repairman for one more of them. And after all, most 'scuttler repairmen — at least, those he had known — were rather shambling, hunched creatures; the error was easy to comprehend, once the circumstances were known.

Poor Cally, Tito thought. Stuck over there, supposedly in safety. What a surprise it must have been, when one of those wooden gliders came sailing past, one day.

It must have been quite a meeting.

11

SEATED IN THE back of the jet-hopper as it made its return flight across the Atlantic, the Peking man in his blue cloth cap and toga-like robe declared, 'My name is Bill Smith.' At least, that was the way the TD linguistics machine handled the utterance. It was the best the circuits could do.

Bill Smith, Sal Heim thought. What an appropriate name the machine's given it! As American as apple pie. He miserably inspected his wristwatch, for the tenth time. Aren't we ever going to get back across this ocean? he wondered. It did not seem so. Time, for him, stood motionless, and he knew who to blame; it was Bill Smith's fault. Riding with *him* in the 'hopper was for Sal Heim a nightmare, yet totally and completely lucidly real.

'Hello, Bill Smith,' Dillingsworth was saying into the mike, now. 'We are glad to know you. We admire your science and efforts as represented by your roads, houses, gliders, ships, motor and clothing. In fact, wherever we look, we see indications of your people's ability.'

The linguistics machine produced a hubbub of grunts, squeals and yips, to which the Peking man listened with slack-jawed intensity; his small, brow-overlain eyes glazed with the effort of paying attention. With a groan, Sal Heim turned away and looked out the 'hopper window instead.

And to think I handed in my resignation over a little matter like the disagreement about George Walt, he reflected. What was that compared with this?

To Jim Briskin, seated beside him, Sal said bitingly, 'I'm certainly going to be interested to hear your next speech. Got any idea what you're going to say, Jim? For instance, about the emigration situation as regards this new development.' He waited, but Jim did not answer; hunched over, Jim somberly scrutinized his interlocked fingers. 'Maybe you could say it's going to be like the Mason-Dixon Line,' Sal continued. 'With them on one side and us on the other. Of course, that's if these Pekes agree. And they might just not.'

'Why should they agree?' Jim said.

'Well, we could offer them the alternative of total annihilation, if Bill Schwarz can see his way clear in that direction.'

'That's out of the question,' Jim said. 'And I know Schwarz would back me up. They've got just as much right to exist as we, especially over here. You know it and I know it and they know it.'

'Is that what you're going to say in your speech? That it's their planet — just after having promised that all the bibs can cross over and become farmers?'

Slowly, Jim said, 'I'm . . . beginning to see what you mean.' His lean face twisted wrathfully. 'Advise me, then. Do your job.'

'This planet,' Sal said, 'will still be able to absorb seventy million bibs. They can fit in on the North American land-mass. But there's going to be friction. People — and those deformed things — are going to get killed. It's going to be roughly a reenactment of the situation when the first white colonists landed in the New World. You see? The Pekes in North America will be driven back, step by step, until the continent is cleared of them; they might as well resign themselves to that, and you might as well, too. I mean, it's inevitable.'

'And then what?'

'And then the trouble—the real trouble—comes. Because sooner or later it's going to occur to some group or some corporation that if we can use North America, we can use Europe and Asia as well. And then the fight that was fought out on both worlds fifty or a hundred thousand years ago is going to take place again, only not with flint hatchets. It'll be with tactical A-bombs and nerve gas and lasers, on our side, and on their side . . .' He paused, ruminating. '. . . with whatever they took out the QB satellite by. Who knows? Maybe in a million and a half years they've managed to stumble over and come up with a source of power we have no knowledge of. Something that's beyond *our* conception. Had you thought of that?'

Jim shrugged.

'And if we press them far enough,' Sal said, 'they'll have to use it on us. They'd have no choice.'

'We can always slam down the door. Close down the nexus by turning off the power supply of the 'scuttler.'

'But by that time there'll be seventy million colonists over there. Can we strand them?'

'Of course not.'

'Then don't talk about "slamming the door down." That's not going to be the answer. The moment the first bib passes over, that's out.' Sal pondered. 'That Bill Smith, back there; for him this is like a ride in a flying saucer would be for one of us. Think what he can tell his playmates when he gets back home. If he ever does.'

'What's a flying saucer?'

Sal said, 'Back in the twentieth century a number of people claimed . . .'

'I remember,' Jim nodded.

'If you were president already,' Sal said, 'if you held formal authority, you could meet with some enormous dignitary from their world, assuming they have a government of some kind.

But right now you're just a private individual; you can't bind this country to anything. And Schwarz, if history repeats itself, won't do a damn thing because he knows he'll soon be out of office. He'll leave it to be dumped in your lap. And by January it'll probably be too late to settle this peacefully.'

'Phil Danville,' Jim said, 'can write me a speech that'll capture this situation and explain it.'

Sal guffawed. 'Like hell he can. *Nobody* is going to be able to capture this situation, especially an intellectual simp like Phil Danville. But let him try. Let's see what Danville can come up with.' Say by tomorrow night, Sal thought. Or the day after, at the very latest.

From his pocket he brought out the itinerary, unfolded it carefully and began to study it.

'I have to speak in Cleveland,' Jim said. 'Tonight.'

In the back of the 'hopper, the Peking man Bill Smith, by means of the linguistics equipment, was saying, '... metal is evil. It belongs inside the Earth with the dead. It is part of the once-was, where everything goes when its time is over.'

'Philosophy,' Sal said in disgust. 'Listen to him.' He jerked his head.

'And that's why you don't build with it?' Dillingsworth asked, speaking into the mike of the machine.

'We have areas we avoid,' Jim said to Sal. 'You'd think twice before making a human skull into a drinking cup and using it every day.'

'Is that what Pekes do?' Sal said, horrified.

'I believe I read that somewhere about them,' Jim said. 'At least their ancestors did. The practice may have disappeared by now.' He added, 'They were cannibals.'

'Great,' Sal said and resumed studying the itinerary. 'That's just what we need to win the election.'

'Schwarz would have brought it out,' Jim said, 'eventually.'

Glancing out the 'hopper window at the ocean below, Sal said, 'I'll be relieved to get out of here. And you won't catch me emigrating. I'd rather do like your folks and give Mars a try, even if I wound up dying of thirst. At least I wouldn't get eaten. And nobody would use my skull for a drinking cup.' He felt severely depressed, meditating about that, and he did his best to reinvolve his attention in the itinerary.

How's the first Negro President of the United States going to go about handling the presence of a planetful of dawn men who've proved themselves capable of constructing a fairly adequate civilization? Sal Heim asked himself. A race that, in theory, shouldn't have been able to get past the flint-chipping stage. But after all, each of us started out chipping flint. What's been proved here is that given time enough . . .

I know I'm right, Sal thought. There isn't a single legal basis on which these Pekes can be denied full rights under our laws — except, of course, that they're not U.S. citizens.

Was that the only barrier? He had to laugh. What a way to stop an invasion of Earth: by denying the invaders citizenship.

But there was, sadly, a joker in that, too. Because U.S. citizens would be emigrating to *this* world, in which the jet-hopper now droned, and in this universe U.S. citizenship had no significance; the Pekes were here first and could prove prior residence. So it would be wise not to raise the issue of citizenship after all . . .

What'll we do, then, Sal asked himself, when our people and the Pekes begin to interbreed? Do you want your daughter to marry a Peke? he asked himself fiercely. Now the Ku Klux Klanners *really* have their job cut out for them.

It was potentially pretty nasty.

At the front door of Pethel Jiffi-scuttler Sales & Service, Stuart Hadley stood leaning on his autonomic broom, watching the people go past. With Dar Pethel gone today, a weight had been lifted from him; he could do what he pleased.

As he stood there mentally magnifying his new status by a few well-chosen daydreams, a slender red-haired shape, full-bosomed and young, all at once strolled up to him, her face stormy. 'They've closed the satellite down,' Sparky said, massive, defeated bitterness.

Awakened. Hadley said, 'W-what?'

'George Walt, that no-good crink, kicked us out this morning. It's all over up there. I have absolutely no idea why. So I came right here to you. What'll we do?' With her toe she nudged a bit of rubbish from the sidewalk into the gutter, glumly.

He reacted. It was superb corto-thalamic response; he was all there, as alert as fine steel. The time had arrived for one of those unique, binding-type decisions which would shape everything to come. 'You set out for the right place, Sparky,' he informed her.

'I know that, Stuart.'

'We'll emigrate.' There it was, the decision.

She glanced sharply up. 'How? Where? To *Mars*?'

'I love you,' Hadley announced to her. He had given it a great deal of thought. The hell with his wife Mary and his job — everything that made up his little routine life.

'Thank you, Stuart,' Sparky said. 'I'm glad you do. But explain where you and I are going to go, for chrissakes, especially where they can't find us.'

'I've got contacts,' Hadley said. 'Believe me, have I got *contacts!* You know where 1 can put us?' In a flash he had it all planned; it leaped fully formed, completed, into his busy brain. 'Get set Sparky.'

'I'm set.' She eyed him.

'Across. To that virgin world Jim Briskin talked about in his

Chicago speech. I can actually — and I'm not kidding you — get us there.'

She was impressed. Her eyes grew large. 'Gee.'

'So go and pack your things,' Hadley instructed her rapidly. 'Give me your vidnumber at your conapt. As soon as I've got the details set up, I'll call you and we'll take off for Washington, D.C.' He explained, 'That's where the nexus is, right now. At TD. That makes it awkward, naturally, but we can still do it.'

'How'll we live over there, Stuart?'

'Let me handle that.' He had worked it all out. It practically blinded him, it was so entire. 'Get going — that damn law that forbids us to meet down here, we don't want to get picked up before we can get away.' And, in addition to the police, he also was thinking about Mary. Every now and then his wife dropped by the store. One glimpse of Sparky and it would be all over; he would be married the rest of his life, possibly two hundred more years. It was not much of a prospect.

On the inside of a match-folder Sparky wrote her vidnumber and gave it to him. He put it away reverently in his billfold and then resumed sweeping with the autonomic broom.

'You're *sweeping*?' Sparky exclaimed. 'I thought we were going to emigrate from Earth; isn't that what you just now said?'

'I'm waiting,' Hadley explained patiently. 'For my top-level contact. Nobody can cross over unless they've got someone they know placed up high, there, at TD. My contact's got carte blanche at TD; he's a wheel. But I have to wait for him to get back here.' He explained, 'He's been at TD all day, on important business.'

'Ding-aling,' Sparky said, awed.

He gave her a swift, brief goodbye kiss and sent her off; her slim figure receded down the sidewalk and then was lost, for the time being, to sight. Hadley swept on, plotting in his mind the last, infinitely tiny details of his scheme. Everything — unfortunately — depended on Darius Pethel. I hope he shows up soon, Hadley said to himself. Before I jump clear out of my skin.

Two hours later, Darius Pethel appeared from the direction of the all day parking lot, his face gray. Mumbling, he passed by Hadley, who still stood out front, and vanished into the store.

Something was bothering Dar, Hadley realized. Bad time to prevail on him, but what choice did he have? He followed after Pethel and found him in the rear office, hanging up his coat.

Pethel said, 'What a day. I wish I could tell you what we ran into over there, but I can't. It's classified; we all agreed. At least we got back here. That's something.' He began rolling up his sleeves and taking an initial look at the day's mail on his desk.

'You've really got those bigshots at TD over a barrel.' Hadley said. 'You could whip that 'scuttler out of there any time, so fast it'd make their heads swim. And then where'd they be? In fact I'd say you're one of the most important persons in the universe, right now.'

Seated at his desk, Pethel eyed him sourly.

Huskily, Stuart Hadley said, 'How about it, Dar?'

'How about what?'

'Set it up so I can go across.'

Pethel stared at him as if he were deranged, and repellently so. 'Get out of here.' He began tearing open his mail.

'I mean it,' Hadley said. 'I'm in love, Dar. I'm leaving. You can get me — the two of us — out of here and across to the other side where we can start our lives over.'

'First of all,' Pethel said, 'you don't know what's over there; you don't have the slightest idea.'

'I know what Jim Briskin said in his speech.'

'Briskin, when he made that speech, hadn't been over there either. Second, Mary would never . . .'

'I don't mean Mary,' Hadley said. 'I'm going with someone else, the first person I ever met who really understood and I could talk to instead of live out a fake role in front of. Sparky and I are going to be the first couple to emigrate and take up a new life in a virgin world half-way down the tube of that Jiffi-scuttler. Don't try to talk me out of it; it's impossible. Write out some sort of note that'll get me into TD's labs. We're depending on you, Dar. Two human lives . . .'

'Aw for god's sake,' Pethel protested. 'How are you going to live over there?'

'How did Cally Vale live?'

'Sands transported one of these old obsolete A-bomb shelters over. Subsurface. Filled with supplies. She lived down in that.'

Hadley said, 'Is the shelter still over there?'

'Of course. What would be the point of transporting it back?'

'We'll live in that, then. Until we can build.'

'What happens when the food in the shelter runs out? Assuming it hasn't already.'

Seating himself on the edge of Dar Pethel's desk, Hadley said, 'I called around. You can pick up one of those colonization units dirt cheap these days; the manufacturers are going broke because virtually nobody is emigrating. They're glad to get rid of one at any price, and the unit contains autonomic fanning equipment, well-drilling rig, basic tools for . . .'

'Okay,' Pethel said, nodding. 'I know what those colonization units contain; I admit one of them can sustain you indefinitely. So you got that part figured out — not bad.'

With fat, sleek pride Hadley said, 'I've even arranged for the unit to be delivered at TD's offices in Washington later today.' He had thought of everything. 'Let's be realistic, Dar; a lot of people are going to be emigrating, and I want to get there first.

I want things to be good for me and Sparky. So will you write out whatever it'll take to get her and me into TD and into that 'scuttler? I ought to have some priority; I was down in the repair department with Erickson when it happened, remember?' He waited. Pethel said nothing. 'Come on,' Hadley said. 'The forces of time and change are running against you, Dar. And you know it, deep down inside.'

'Yes, but they always have,' Pethel murmured. He got a sheet of paper, brought out his pen. 'Are you really in — how did you describe it? — *love* with her?'

Hadley said, 'On my mother's honor.'

Wincing, Pethel began to write.

'I'll never forget you for this,' Hadley said. 'And I hate like hell to leave you stranded with no sales manager . . . but it can't be helped; she's depending on me.' He explained, 'George Walt, you know, those two mutants who own the satellite, they closed everything down.'

Pethel ceased writing, lifted his head. 'No kidding.' He scowled. 'I wonder what that means. I wonder what they have in mind.'

'Who cares what they have in mind?' Hadley said fervently. 'I'm getting out of here.'

'But I'm not,' Pethel pointed out. He slowly resumed writing, deep in frowning thought.

When Leon Turpin, chairman of the board of directors of Terran Development, heard the news about the Pekes he was fit to be tied. How can we get any new industrial techniques out of *that?* he asked himself. Dawn men don't have anything on the ball, technologically speaking.

'Flint axes,' Turpin spat out disappointedly. 'So that's what's over there; that's what hopped out of that childish glider. And we've expended a QB satellite, seven million dollars.' Of course there were still mineral rights. The Pekes, according to Don Stanley's report, definitely did not mine; therefore, everything below the soil remained intact.

But that was not enough. Turpin yearned for more. There *had* to be more. His mind reverted to the fallen satellite. They did manage to knock that out, he realized, and we're still having trouble doing that.

Across from him Don Stanley shifted about restlessly in his chair. 'If you'd like to see the Peking man we brought back, this Bill Smith, as the linguistics machine calls him —'

'If I want to see a Peking man,' Turpin said, 'I'll look in the *Britannica*. That's where they belong, Stanley, not walking around on the face of the globe as if they owned it. But I guess it can't be helped, not at this late date.' From his desk he picked up a letter. 'Here's a young couple, Art and Rachael Chaffy, that want to emigrate over there. The first of a horde. Why not? Call them up and tell them to come by, and we'll let them go across.' He tossed the letter toward Don Stanley.

'Should I explain to them the risks?'

Turpin shrugged. 'I don't see why you should; that's not our business. Let them find out the hard way. Colonists are supposed to be hardy and brave. At least they used to be, in my time. Back in the twentieth century, when we first started landing on the planets. This certainly is no worse than that; in fact it's considerably better.'

'You've got a point, Mr Turpin.' Stanley folded the letter and placed it in his breast pocket.

The intercom on Turpin's desk said, 'Mr T, there's an official from the U.S. Department of Special Public Welfare here to see you. It's Mr Thomas Rosenfeld, commissioner of the department.'

Cabinet level, Turpin said to himself. A big man. Capable of setting policy. He said to the intercom, 'Send Mr Rosenfeld in.' To Stanley he said, 'You know what this is going to be?'

'Bibs,' Stanley said.

'I can't make up my mind whether to tell him or not,' Turpin said. The news about the Pekes would very soon, of course, begin to seep out; it was a temporary secret only. But still, that was better than nothing. The party had just returned from the other side, and the media people who had been along could not possibly have released the news through their services so soon. Rosenfeld, then, did not know; he could assume that. And could deal with the man accordingly.

A tall, red-haired man, well-dressed, entered Turpin's office, smiling. 'Mr Turpin? What a pleasure. President Schwarz asked me to drop by here for a little while and sort of chat with you. Sound you out, as it were. Is that an original Ramon Cadiz you have there on the wall behind you?' Rosenfeld walked over to inspect it. 'White on white. His best period.'

'I'd give the painting to you,' Turpin said, 'but it was a gift to me. I know you'll understand.' He lied in his teeth, but why not? Why, for purposes of mere etiquette, should he give away a costly work of art? It made no sense.

Rosenfeld said, 'How's your defective 'scuttler functioning? Still as defective as ever? We're very interested in it. We were, even before Jim Briskin's speech . . . President Schawz was exceptionally quick — even for him — to spot the potentialities in this. I don't believe anyone else is able to reach a major decision as efficiently as he.'

This was odd, in view of the fact that no way existed by which Schwarz could have known about the breakthrough prior to Briskin's speech, Turpin realized. However, he let this pass. Politics was politics.

Don Stanley spoke up. 'How many sleepers do you have in the fedgov warehouses, Mr Rosenfeld?'

'Well,' Rosenfeld said drily, 'the figure generally given is close to seventy million. But actually the true number at this date is more like one hundred million.' He smiled a wry, humorless smile that was more a grimace than anything else.

Whistling, Stanley said, 'That's a lot.'

'Yes,' Rosenfeld agreed. 'We admit it. Domestically speaking, it's the number one headache here in Washington. Of course as you very well know, this administration inherited it from the last.'

'You want us to put your hundred million bibs through into this alternate Earth?' Turpin spoke up, weary of formalities.

'If the situation is such that . . .'

'We can do it,' Turpin said shortly. 'But you understand our role in this is simply a technologic one. We provide the means of conveyance to this other Earth, but we make no warranty as to the conditions that obtain over there. We're not anthropologists or sociologists or whoever it is that knows about such things.'

Rosenfeld nodded. 'That's understood. We're not going to try to compel you to produce any given set of conditions, over there. Your job, as you say, is merely to get the persons across, and the rest is up to them. The government takes the identical position regarding itself; we put forth no warranty, either. This will be strictly on an as-is basis. If the settlers don't like what they find, they can return.'

To himself Turpin thought acutely: So Schwarz doesn't actually care what happens to them after they emigrate. He just wants those warehouses empty and the enormous finanacial drain involved abolished.

'As to our costs . . .' Turpin began.

'We've worked out a proposed schedule,' Rosenfeld said, digging into his briefcase. 'Per capita and then extrapolated. Basing this on the figure of one hundred million persons, this is what we feel would be an equitable return for your corporation.' He slid a folded document to Leon Turpin and sat back to wait.

Turpin, examining the figure, blanched.

Coming around behind him, Don Stanley also looked. He grunted and said in a strained voice, 'That's a good deal of money, Mr Rosenfeld.'

'It's a good deal of a problem.' Rosenfeld said, candidly.

Glancing up, Turpin said, 'It's actually worth that much to you?'

'Our costs in the Dept of SPW are . . .' Rosenfeld gestured. 'Let's simply say they're excessive.'

But that doesn't explain this figure, Turpin decided. However, I know what does. If you can get the ball rolling right away, get the bibs started on their trek to the alter-Earth, *you'll have deprived Jim Briskin of his major appeal.* Why vote for Briskin when the incumbent is already shipping the bibs across as rapidly as possible?

As rapidly as possible. Turpin thought suddenly: But just how rapidly is that? To Don Stanley he said, 'How fast can full-grown human beings be put through that rent?'

'It would have to be one at a time,' Stanley said, after a thoughtful pause. 'Since it's not very large. In fact, as you probably recall, you have to stoop down to get through.'

With pencil and paper Turpin began to calculate.

Allowing five seconds for each person — which was not a great deal — the time involved in conveying one hundred million bibs across would be approximately twenty years.

Seeing the figures, Don Stanley said, 'But they don't care; they're asleep. For them twenty years is . . .'

'But I imagine Mr Rosenfeld cares,' Turpin said caustically.

'Is *that* how long it would require?' Rosenfeld looked a little unnerved. 'That is a long time.'

Turpin reflected that Bill Schwarz, by the time the job had been completed, would have been out of office sixteen years. Probably totally forgotten, to boot. So there was no use trying to sell the fedgov on the idea. The time element would simply have to be cut down.

To Don Stanley, Turpin said, 'Can that rent be enlarged?'

Pondering, Stanley answered, 'Probably. Increased grid voltage or oscillation within the field as it . . .'

'I don't want to know how,' Turpin said. 'I just want to see it done.' If two persons could pass through simultaneously, the time would be cut to ten years. And four at once, only five years. That might satisfy the politicians in the White House.

'Five years would be acceptable,' Rosenfeld said, when he had looked over Turpin's figures.

'We'll finalize on that basis, then,' Don Stanley said. But he had a worried expression on his face, and Turpin knew why. Don was thinking, *Can* it be done? Can we enlarge the rent that much?

Rising, Rosenfeld said, 'Good enough. Legal people from my department will draw up the contract in the next day or so, and procurement will go through the process of validating it. Red tape — we can't seem to get away from it. But this will give you time to implement your engineering changes.'

'It was nice meeting you, Mr Rosenfeld,' Turpin said, as they shook hands. 'I presume we'll see you again from time to time as this matter is expedited.'

'I find it highly rewarding, working with you, sir,' Rosenfeld said. 'And I admire your taste in art; that's only the second Ramon Cadiz I've seen this year. Good day, Mr Turpin. Mr Stanley.'

The door closed after Rosenfeld.

Presently Don Stanley said, 'They like being in office.'

'Everybody likes being in office,' Turpin said. 'We call that human nature.' He wondered what the government would do when the news about the Pekes appeared in every homeopape in the country. Rescind the contract? Abandon the whole idea?

He doubted it. Either Schwarz did this or he lost in November; it was as simple as that Pekes or no Pekes. Of course, the president would send a few Marine commando units to accompany the bibs, to make certain that all was in order. Alter-Earth might require an interval of pacifying, to say the least. But it could be done. Turpin had no doubt of it.

And anyhow that was not TD's problem—TD had its technological hands full already. Enlarging the rent in the 'scuttler might very well prove to be impossible, at least within the time available to TD's technicians.

But I want this contract, Leon Turpin said to himself. I want it very badly, enough to do everything I can to acquire it. Perhaps the solution is to fabricate another Jiffi-scuttler, identical to the one downstairs, hopefully malfunctioning in the same way. Or two or five or even ten of them, with bibs passing in single file through each, in unending lines.

What about equipment? Turpin asked himself suddenly. Rosenfeld had not expressed himself in that area. Was the government going to turn these people loose in an alien world with no hardware? Without proper machinery the colony on the other side would be nothing more than a huge DP camp. To function at all, the colony had to be self-sustaining; that was obvious to anyone who took the trouble to think about it ten minutes. And it would take time, a good deal of time, to ferry across sufficient gear for one hundred million people; the logistics of it would be incredible. It would be something like thirty-three times the problem of supply on D-day, back in World War Two. The government was out of its mind. The policy planners were so enmeshed in the political significance of the alter-Earth that they had lost sight of factual reality.

It could easily become the grandest confusion in recorded times.

But I refuse to worry about that, Leon Turpin reminded himself. It's not my responsibility; mine's discharged in the drayage. If things get too far out of hand too soon, Schwarz will be bounced right out of office and the burden will fall on Jim Briskin or whatever his name is. And that's just where it ought to be, because it was his speech that got this all started.

'Get everyone downstairs assembled in one spot where they can hear you,' Turpin instructed Don Stanley.

'How much time do you estimate we've got?' Stanley asked.

'Days. Merely days. There's a presidential campaign going on, or had that slipped your mind? We've already given Briskin a boost by letting Frank Woodbine talk us into conveying him over there; now let's see what we can do for Bill Schwarz.' And what we can do for Schwarz is a good deal more than we did for Briskin. Which was, in itself, rather substantial.

Don Stanley departed, to make the situation known to the experts on level one. As he passed out through the office door one of Leon Turpin's many secretaries entered. 'Mr Turpin, there's a young couple on floor five who sent this up to you; they said you should see it at once.' The secretary added, 'It's from Mr Pethel.'

'Who's Mr Pethel?' The name did not ring a bell.

'The owner of the Jiffi-scuttler, sir. The one downstairs in the lab; you know, the *important* one.' She presented him with the message.

Opening it, Leon Turpin saw at a glance that it consisted of a request for him to permit the young couple, Mr and Mrs Hadley, to make use of Pethel's 'scuttler in order to emigrate to alter-Earth. Time was of the essence, for reasons Pethel did not choose to state.

'All right,' Turpin said to the girl, 'I have no objection and we have to cater to this Pethel person to some extent.' As he laid the message on his desk, he once more noticed the application from the other young couple, Art and Rachael Chaffy. That's right, he remembered. Don was supposed to call them, but I guess he forgot in all the excitement. Well, he can do it later. He's got their letter with him.

The Chaffys and the Hadleys can compete, Turpin reflected, as to who becomes the first American family to emigrate to alter-Earth. I suppose there should be some publicity attached to this. Homeopape reporters, TV newsmen and the like. President Schwarz cutting a big blue ribbon hung across the entrance hoop of the 'scuttler. Or perhaps a bottle of champagne swung against the side of the 'scuttler and an heroic name given it.

To the secretary he said, 'Ask the Hadleys to come up here to my office.'

Several minutes later she returned and with her came a blond, genial-looking young man and a fabulously-attractive red-headed girl who seemed sheepish and ill-at-ease.

'Sit down,' Leon Turpin said in a friendly voice.

'Mr. Pethel's my boss,' Hadley said. 'Rather, my ex-boss. I had to quit in order to emigrate.' He and 'Mrs Hadley' seated themselves. 'This is the greatest moment in our entire lives. We're going to start a new life.' Hadley squeezed his 'wife's' hand. 'Right?'

'Yes,' she murmured almost inaudibly, nodding. She did not look at Turpin directly, and he wondered why.

I've seen this girl somewhere before, Turpin realized. But where?

'Are you fully equipped?' he asked the Hadleys.

Briskly, Hadley gave him a long list of items they were taking; it sounded complete, if not ornate. Turpin wondered idly how they expected to lug it all across. Nobody on floor one would be offering them a hand; that was certain.

'Children,' Leon Turpin said, 'Terran Development is glad to contribute to a new awakening, both metaphorically and quite literally, of the young people of America . . .' And then, abruptly, he remembered where he met full-breasted young Mrs Hadley before. He had gotten her at the Golden Door Moments of Bliss satellite. After all, he visited it twice a week, had done so ever since it had been built.

This is really terribly appropriate, Turpin said to himself, hiding his glee. The first couple to emigrate to the new world consists of a customer of the Golden Door satellite escaping with one of Thisbe Olt's girls. Too bad this could not be made public. It was delightful.

'I wish you two luck,' Leon Turpin said, and giggled.

12

WITHIN ONE WEEK the initial collection of bibs passed through the Jiffi-scuttler and into another world entirely, to virtually everyone's satisfaction. On TV the country watched it and in person Leon Turpin, President Schwarz, the Republican-Liberal candidate James Briskin, and Darius Pethel — who owned the 'scuttler — and other pertinent notables looked on with a galaxy of emotions, most of them concealed.

The darn fools, Dar Pethel thought as he watched the steady line of men and women trudge past the entrance hoop. It made *him* sick to his stomach, and he turned and walked to the far end of TD's lab, to light a cigarette. Don't they know what's going to happen to them on the other side? Don't they care? Doesn't *anyone* care?

I ought to close it down, Pethel said to himself. It's my 'scuttler. And I've decided I don't want it used for this, not now, not after my trip over there, that 'hopper ride back across the Atlantic with Bill Smith.

He wondered where Bill Smith, the Peking man, was now. Perhaps at Yale Psychiatric Institute or some such august place, being put through aptitude and profile tests, one after another. And of course being subjected to relentless questioning regarding the ingredients of his culture.

Some of Bill Smith's testimony had leaked to the homeo-papes. The Pekes had not, for instance, discovered glass. Rubber, too, was unknown to them, as were electricity, gunpowder, and, of course, atomic energy. But, more mysteriously, both clocks and the steam engine had never been stumbled onto or developed by the Pekes, and Dar Pethel could make no sense out of that. In fact, their entire society was an enigma to him.

However, one thing was certain: there had been no Thomas Edison on alter-Earth. Phonographs, light bulbs, and, for that matter, the telephone and even the ancient telegraph, were absent. What inventions they did have — for example the technique of laying crushed rock roads — had been developed over enormously long periods, microscopically elaborated by each generation mosaic-style. Except for the odd, complex compressor and turbine system, nothing seemed to have come to the Pekes in a single creative leap.

The device by which the QB satellite had been knocked off remained a mystery; Bill Smith knew nothing about it, according to the homeopapes, and knew nothing even of the satellite. The linguistics machine appeared to be unable to clarify the situation.

Jim Briskin, as he also watched, found himself dwelling on the gloomier aspects of the situation.

Where we made our mistake, he decided, was in not coming to some kind of rapprochement with the Pitecanthropi. It should have been done before a single emigrant crossed over . . . now, of course, it's too late. But of course President Schwarz had to proceed swiftly if this was to become a way of stealing Jim Briskin's thunder. Both men knew this. In his situation, Jim mulled, I probably would have done the same.

But that doesn't make it any less lethal.

Standing beside him, Sal Heim murmured, 'When do you

think they'll be streaming back? Or will they be able to *get* back?'

'Cally Vale stood it. Alone. Possibly they can adapt; it's certainly more viable an environment than Mars.' In fact, there was no comparison. Mars was utterly impossible and everyone knew it. 'It all depends on the reaction of the Peking people.' And, he reflected, since the Schwarz administration couldn't wait to find that out, we'll have to learn it the hard way. In terms of the loss of human life.

'What I'm trying to figure out,' Sal murmured, 'is whether the public still identifies you with this or whether Schwarz has succeeded in. . . .'

'Even if you knew that,' Jim said, 'you wouldn't know anything. Because we don't know yet what the upshot of this mass migration is going to be, and I have a feeling that when we find out it won't matter who gets the credit for it; we'll all be in the pot together.'

Sal said, 'I heard an interesting rumor on my way here. You're aware that George Walt have been missing since they shut down the Golden Door. According to this rumor . . .' Sal chuckled. 'They emigrated.'

Feeling a pervasive, shocked chill, Jim said, 'They what? To alter-Earth, you mean?'

'Right through this 'scuttler, here, that we're looking at.'

'But that ought to be easy to check on. If George Walt had passed through, TD's engineers would certainly remember; they could hardly mistake George Walt for anybody else.' He was now deeply disturbed. 'I'll see what Leon Turpin has to say about it.'

'Don't be so sure George Walt would be noticed,' Sal said. 'He, the actual living brother, may have carried his synthetic twin over in dissembled form, identified as maintenance and colonizing equipment; everyone who goes across carries *something,* some of them a couple tons.'

'Why would George Walt emigrate?' In fact, why had they shut the satellite down? Nobody had been able to explain that to his satisfaction, although a number of theories had been floating around, the central one being that George Walt anticipated Jim's election and realized that their day had virtually arrived.

'Maybe the Pekes will take care of them,' Sal offered. 'They would be rather a disheartening apparition, appearing in their midst; the Pekes might take it as a bad omen and cast the two of them back here in pieces.'

'Who would be able to find this out?' Jim said.

'You mean what George Walt are up to on the other side — assuming they're there? Perhaps Tito Cravelli.'

'How would Tito know? He doesn't have any contacts among the Peking people.'

Sal said, 'Tito keeps tabs on everything.'

'Not on this,' Jim disagreed. 'George Walt, if they've crossed over, have gone where we can't scrutinize them; that's the cold, hard truth and we might as well face it.' Broodingly he said, 'If I was positive they'd crossed over, I think I'd seriously plead with TD to shut the 'scuttler down, To keep them bottled up over there, for the rest of eternity.'

'Are you that much afraid of George Walt?'

'Sometimes I am. Especially very late at night. I am right now, hearing about this.' He moved a little away from Sal Heim, feeling depressed. 'I thought we were through with George Walt,' he said.

'Through with them? Without killing them?' Sal laughed.

I guess in the final analysis I'm not very bright, Jim Briskin said to himself glumly. We should have finished it, up there at the satellite, when we almost had them. Instead we chose to shuffle naively back to Terra, for what seemed a good idea at the time: a cup of hot syntho-coffee.

Now, it did not seem very brilliant. The passage of even a little time was a great edifier.

Sal said sardonically, 'Hell, Jim, maybe you won their respect by being so charitable.' He obviously did not think so. Far from it.

'You're a great second-guesser,' Jim said, with bitterness. 'Where were you with your advice then?'

Sal said quietly, 'Nobody expected them to do something so radical as close the Golden Door. What happened up there on the satellite that day must really have shaken them.'

Coming up beside him, ancient Leon Turpin leered happily and cackled, 'Well, Briskin, or whatever you call yourself, that's the first batch of bibs. Historic, isn't it? Makes you feel young again, doesn't it? Say something. At least, smile.' To Sal he said, 'Is he always this solemn?'

'Jim runs deep, Mr Turpin,' Sal said. 'You have to get accustomed to it.'

'Just wait until we get that rent enlarged,' Turpin wheezed. 'My boys have been on it all week and tonight they're going to hook up an entirely different power source; it's all plotted out, rechecked dozens of times. By tomorrow morning, we should have a hole two to three times bigger. And then we can really hustle them through. Zip.' He made a quick gesture.

'Have you made thorough provision,' Jim said, 'to receive them back in the event something goes wrong on the other side?'

'Well,' Leon Turpin conceded, 'the 'scuttler will be turned off most of the night as the boys work it over. Nobody can pass through then, of course. But we weren't expecting any trouble. At least not so soon.'

Sal and Jim glanced at each other.

'President Schwarz said it would be agreeable,' Turpin added. 'After all, our contract is with the Dept of SPW. We're acting well within the law. There's nothing that *compels* us to keep the 'scuttler running at all times.'

God pity those colonists, Jim Briskin said to himself, if anything does go wrong tonight.

'They know about the Pekes,' Turpin protested. 'It's been in the papes constantly; nothing's been concealed from them: as soon as they were revived the situation was explained to them in detail. Nobody *forced* them to go.'

Jim said, 'They were given the choice of going across or being put back to sleep.' He knew that for a fact; Tito had informed him.

'As far as I'm concerned,' Leon Turpin said sulkily, 'those people are over there voluntarily. And any risk they're taking —'

You skunk, Jim Briskin thought.

It was going to be a long night. At least for him.

At eleven P.M. Tito Cravelli received from one of his almost infinite number of paid contacts a piece of news which did not resemble anything he had ever picked up before. Frankly, he did not know whether to laugh or rush to the tocsin; it was simply too goddam peculiar.

He mixed himself a whiskey sour in the kitchen of his conapt and pondered. The datum had reached him by a circuitous route; initially it had been piped from a TD exploration team on the other side of the 'scuttler nexus, prior to the shutting-down of the 'scuttler, and from there to Bohegian, whereupon Earl had of course relayed it to him. Was it possibly a gag? If he could regard it that way, it would be a distinct relief. But he could not afford to; it might be bona fide. And in that case . . .

Back in the living room, he dialed Jim Briskin's number. 'Listen to this,' Cravelli said, when he had Jim on the vidscreen. He did not bother to apologize for waking Jim up; that hardly mattered. 'See what you can make out of this. George Walt is with the Pekes, at their population center in northern Europe. TD's field corps believes they made contact with the Pekes somewhere in North America, and the Pekes then transported them across the Atlantic.'

'So quickly?' Jim said. 'I thought they had nothing better than slow surface ships.'

'Here's the substance of it. The Pekes have installed George Walt at their capital and are worshipping them as a god.'

There was silence.

Finally Jim said, 'How — did the TD field corps find this out?'

'From parleys with North American Pekes. They've been palavering continually; you know that. Those linguistics machines have been droning on night and day. The Pekes are — dazzled. Well, weren't we a little in awe of George Walt ourselves? It's not so odd when you think of it. I'd make book that George Walt went there anticipating some such reaction as that; they probably did some groundwork in advance.'

Jim said cyptically, 'Another one of Sal's predictions bites the dust.' He looked weary. 'Cravelli, you know we're over our head. Schwarz is over *his* head. If someone suggested shutting —'

'And strand those people over there?'

'They can be brought back tomorrow morning. And then it could be shut down.'

'There's too much momentum behind it now,' Cravelli pointed out. You can't turn off a mass movement like that. In Dept of SPW warehouses all over the United States, they're rousing the sleepers right and left. Assembling equipment, arranging transportation to Washington, D.C. —'

'I'll call Schwarz,' Jim said.

'He won't listen to you. He'll think you're just trying to regain a primary relationship to the project, a relationship which he inherited by moving so quickly. Schwarz has the initiative now, Jim, not you. His whole political life depends on pushing those bibs across as fast as possible. Fix yourself a great big stiff type drink. That's what I did. And then go back to bed. I'll talk to you again in the morning. Maybe in the light of day we can hatch something out.' But he didn't think so.

Jim said, 'I'll talk to Leon Turpin, then.'

'Ha! Turpin and Schwarz are interlaced through that lush contract let to TD through Rosenfeld; it's a masterpiece. You can't offer TD that kind of money — I hear it involves billions of dollars, and all TD has to do is keep the 'scuttler going, just stand there and pump power to it.' Cravelli added, 'And enlarge the aperture, I understand. But that ought to be easy enough; they've been studying it for the last week.' In fact they had probably already accomplished it. 'I'm going back to my drink, now. And then I'm going to fix another and then . . .'

'There's one man who can stop this. The owner of the 'scuttler. I met him on that trip across the Atlantic. Darius Pethel, in Kansas City.'

'Yes, he *claims* it as part of his inventory. But dammit, Jim, are you really sure you want to shut down the 'scuttler and stop emigration? *It would be the end of you politically.* Sal must have told you that already.'

Woodenly, Jim nodded. 'Yes. Sal told me.'

'Don't do anything tonight.'

'We're in the grip of fate,' Jim said. 'We *can't* do anything; we've started something bigger than all of us put together. We may be seeing the end of the human race.'

'*Humanum est errare?*' Cravelli said, assuming he was joking. But was he? 'You don't mean that,' Cravelli said, stricken. 'I hate that kind of talk; it's morbid and defeatist and ten other things, all of them bad. That acceptance speech you gave at the nominating convention; it was cut out of the same lousy cloth. Sal ought to give you a good swift kick.'

'I believe what I believe,' Jim said.

At four A.M. the augmented power supply had been coupled to the Jiffi-scuttler; supervising the work, Don Stanley gave the go-ahead signal to start the 'scuttler back up. It had been off now for six and a half hours. His fingers crossed, Stanley tensely smoked his cigarette and waited as the entrance hoop gradually flared into unusual, pale-yellow brilliance, at least four times as bright as before.

Beside him, Bascolm Howard, who had strolled in to watch, said, 'It certainly caught right away. No hesitation there.'

'It really shines,' Stanley murmured. God, suppose we're overloading it he thought. Suppose it heats up too much and burns out. But the engineers who had done the work had assured *him* that the load was within the safe tolerance. And he had to go by what they said.

'Tired?' Howard asked him.

'Darn right.' Stanley felt irritable. 'I ought to be home in bed.' We all should be, he said to himself. I'll be glad when they've run the final tests on this and it's ready to go back into operation.

A senior engineer hopped into the tube of the 'scuttler and disappeared from sight. Stanley dropped his cigarette to the lab floor and savagely ground it out. Now we learn the truth, he realized. We get the poop, whether we've failed or been successful.

Minutes passed.

Reappearing, the engineer called to him. 'Mr Stanley, would you come here, please?'

Stanley, on rubber legs, made his way to the tube. 'How is it inside there?'

'The rent's big, now. Three and a half, maybe four times greater.'

Feeling limp as tension throughout his body lessened, Stanley said, 'Fine. Now we can go home where we belong.'

'I want you to look through the rent,' the engineer said.

'Why?' He did not see the point.

The engineer said, 'Just look, okay? For chrissake, will you please *look*, Mr Stanley?'

He looked.

Through the rent in the tube wall he saw, not a grassy meadow and ultramarine sky, no white flowers with buzzing, lazy bees tackling them. And he saw no sign of people. None of the tons of equipment which had been passed through the rent. No tents. No temporary septic tanks. No improvised food kitchens or overhead lighting. Instead he saw — and could not at first accept that he saw — a marshlike expanse, gray with mist and the hollow croakings of some distant birds. He saw reeds poking through the gummy, yellow water which lay in pools. A snake moved suddenly, twisting its path through the stagnant debris. And over to the right, some small living creature with a naked tail dropped to safety in the dense shadows beneath a cracked, hairy mass of roots.

The air smelled of decay and silent, utter death.

Pulling back into the 'scuttler tube, Stanley said hoarsely, 'It's not the same place.'

His chief engineer nodded mutely.

'It's a swamp,' Stanley said. 'My god, what kind of catastrophe is this? Can you make any sense out of it? We better get the original power supply right back on; you evidently can't increase the load and get the same results only more so, instead you get this, whatever it is.' He took one more look. All his determination was required merely to *see* it, let alone venture through the rent and actually into it. 'I think I understand,' he said, muttering to himself. 'There's not just one alter-Earth, parallel universe or whatever you call it; there's several, and why we didn't deal that factor into our planning I'll never know. We'll never make that mistake again.'

'I agree,' his engineer said, beside him, also looking.

'You think we can restore the original power supply and make contact again with where we dumped those people?'

'We can try.'

'We've got to,' Stanley said. 'You know who'll get the rap; it'll be us. Start work immediately; we'll work the rest of the night.' God, he thought. What'll I tell old man Turpin? Nothing. If we can get this patched up again we'll see it's forgotten forever. Like it never happened.

'I'm not thinking about us getting the blame,' the senior engineer said to him. 'I'm thinking about those people, especially those women, stranded there.'

'They'll be okay! They've got supplies; they went there to colonize, so let them colonize. It was their idea to go across, they knew they were taking a risk. It was their responsibility. So tough tubes.' He drew himself back into the 'scuttler, shaking. 'Wow, what a hell of a sight. I can't see colonizing *there*. You think you'd like to live there, Hal?'

'No, Mr Stanley,' the engineer said. He rose to his feet stiffly, waved to the team standing before the entrance hoop. 'Shut it off!'

The power died. Stanley walked back out of the tube and over to Howard. 'Now we have to take apart the whole damn thing again and fix it back up the way it was,' he said bitterly. 'What lousy luck. And it's going to take twenty years to get those millions of bibs through; President Schwarz'll never buy that. That's the end of that contract. That voids it automatically.' And to think we worked six and a half hours for this, he said to himself.

Something appeared at the mouth of the tube.

Stanley saw it, but, even as he saw it, the shadow-like substance vanished.

'Who has a laser pistol?' he said.

'Get a laser pistol,' Howard said. Evidently he had seen it, too. 'It must have followed you. Come over from the other side. Before the power was turned off.'

'It's just an insect,' Stanley said. 'Some miserable thing that flew up out of that swamp.' I know that's all it is, he said to himself. It's got to be. 'For chrissakes, somebody kill it!' he said, looking around. Where had it gone? Not back into the tube, but out into the room.

From within the tube, the senior engineer said loudly, 'Mr Stanley, the rent never shut down.'

'That's absolutely impossible,' Stanley said. 'The power's off.' He ran back into the tube, found the engineer crouched down by the rent. Once more Stanley saw across, into the world of the swamp, the decaying landscape of doomed, collapsing ruin. His senior engineer was right; it was still there.

'I can think of only one explanation,' the engineer said to Stanley. 'It must be that it's maintained by a power source on the other side, because you know no power's coming to it from here; that's for sure.'

Stanley said, 'Did you see something that slipped through just now? Something alive?'

'Only for a second. But I thought it went back.'

'It didn't go back,' Stanley said. 'It's out somewhere in the lab, in the TD building, on our side, and now more are going to come across because we can't shut down this damn rent. Maybe we can block it somehow. Can you put a barrier right up? I don't care what it's made out of, just as long as it's good and solid.'

'We'll get on it right away,' the engineer said and scrambled to his feet.

What kind of power source could exist there on the other side? Stanley asked himself. There in that brackish, desolate swamp . . . it's as if it were waiting. But how could it know we'd show up? How could it possibly have been expecting us?'

When he made his way out of the tube once more, Howard said to him, 'It's still somewhere in the room. I can feel it, but I'll be darned if I can see it. It's like it just merged with everything on this side, just sort of — you know, whatever it saw here.'

Don Stanley tried to remember when he had felt such fear. Not for a long time. Had he ever reacted this way to anything in his life before?

Once, he recalled. Years ago. He had felt the same fright when as he had felt now, seeing this dark, pervasive substance scuttle into his world from the other side. I was eighteen, he said to himself. Just a kid. It was my first visit to the Golden Door satellite.

It had been when he had first seen George Walt.

Since it was impossible to close the rent, Don Stanley decided, they were going to have to make the attempt to subject the dimly-lit swamp world to some kind of ordered scrutiny. Taking full responsiblity, he ordered a QB observation satellite brought to the lab with launching equipment. Before the barrier had been erected by TD's engineers he had sent the satellite across and had watched as it shot up into the murky, ominous sky.

Reports from the orbiting satellite began to arrive almost at once, and he seated himself with Howard and started methodically to go over them. The time was five-thirty A.M. Much too early to awaken Leon Turpin, he realized. We'll just have to go on as we are, for at least another two hours.

The planet — and he felt no surprise in learning this — was Earth. But the stellar chart which the satellite recorded on the dark side contained data which was totally unexpected. For a long time he and Howard sat together conferring, to be certain there had been no error. There had not. By six-thirty in the morning, Stanley was sure of the situation, sure enough to have Leon Turpin woken up at his home on Long Island.

The QB satellite, this time, was orbiting an Earth in what was, for their world, a century in the future.

'You realize what this implies, don't you?' he said to Howard.

'This could still be the same alter-Earth. The one we sent our colonists onto. Only we're seeing it a hundred years later.' Abruptly Howard shivered. 'Then what became of their colonizing efforts? No trace at all? *After all, the satellite is picking up lights on the dark side in exactly the same locations as before.*'

'I'll be glad when Turpin gets here,' Stanley said. The responsibility had become too much for him; he wanted out. Obviously, the colonization attempt had failed. But he simply refused to face it. It can't be the same Earth, he repeated again and again to himself. It's just got to be a totally different one.

Something terrible must have taken place between our colonists and the Pekes.

At seven fifteen A.M., Leon Turpin arrived, perfectly shaved, washed, dressed, and in absolute control of himself.

'Have you sent dredging equipment across?' he asked Stanley as the two of them stood by the partly-completed concrete barrier, looking out across the swamp.

'What for?' Stanely said.

Turpin's face twitched. 'To look for remains of our campsite. This is the same spot, isn't it? There's been no movement in space; this is where our colonists set up their base a century ago. There ought to be all kinds of junk, if we dig down far enough, down to the hundred-year level. Tell them to get started right away.'

It took only two hours for the dredges to locate and bring up an aluminum canteen and then a rusted, corroded, slime-drenched U.S. Army laser rifle. And, after that . . .

Skeletons. First one which they identified as a human male and then a smaller one, possibly that of a female.

Turpin signalled for the dredging to cease.

'Beyond any reasonable doubt, this was our campsite,' Turpin said, presently. 'We've proved that, to my satisfaction at least,' The others nodded; no one spoke, however, and they did not look directly at one another. 'Perhaps it's possible to view this as a tremendous break,' Turpin said. 'We know now not to send any more colonists across; we know what's going to happen to them. They're going to perish right here at the campsite without having even . . .'

'They were slaughtered,' Stanley interrupted, *'because* we didn't send any more across. The first group wasn't large enough to hold off the Pekes; it's obvious that the Pekes are responsible for this massacre. What else could have happened to them?'

'Disease,' Howard said, after a pause. 'We never took time to make thorough studies of viruses and protozoa over there, as we should have. We were in such a goddam hurry to rush them across.'

'If we had kept sending them across,' Stanley persisted, 'in a steady flow, the Pekes wouldn't have been able to mow them down. My god, those colonists suddenly found themselves cut off from us, stranded there with no way to get back, abandoned by us . . .' He broke off. 'We never should have tinkered with the power supply. That's where we made our mistake.'

Howard said, 'I wonder what we'll find when we get the original power supply hooked back up.' He jerked his head toward the group of TD engineers laboring to disconnect the larger source. 'In a few more hours they'll have it back the way it was. Presumably we'll find ourselves facing the original rent, the original conditions; we'll be back in contact with our campsite, then, and if necessary we can march them all back here to this side again. Every last one of them.'

'But,' Stanley said almost inaudibly, 'you're leaving a factor out. The nexus to this swamp world hasn't gone away; it's either self-maintaining or some force on the other side is underwriting it . . . in any case it seems to be there for good. *Things are never going to be as they were;* we can't reestablish the original situation. We'll never see those colonists again. And we might as well get used to that idea. I say, go ahead and hook up the first, smaller power source again, but don't expect anything.' To Leon Turpin, he said, 'I've been here all night. Can I go home and go to bed for a few hours? I can't keep my eyes open.'

Turpin said raspingly, 'Don't you want to be here when . . .'

'You're just not facing it,' Stanley said. 'When I wake up, six or ten or fifteen hours from now, the situation's going to be exactly as it is right now. We'll be looking across at that swamp world, and it'll be staring right back at us. I'll tell you what we've got to do. Somebody — and I don't mean just another atavistic, simple-minded robot-type dredge — some brilliant human individual has got to go across there into that swamp world and locate the power source that's keeping this nexus alive. And then he's got to blow it to bits or, at the very least, dismantle it.' Stanley added, 'And then — and this may be almost impossible — someone's got to find out *who* established that power source in the first place. And how they knew we were coming.'

After a pause Leon Turpin said, 'Howard tells me that in the first few moments of operation with the augmented power source, something came through, some living creature. Is that true?'

Don Stanley sighed wearily. 'I thought so at the time. Now I think I was out of my mind; I was simply just too scared by what

I saw. I must have realized right away that we had lost those colonists forever.' He walked unsteadily toward the exit door of the lab. 'I'll see you a few hours from now. After I've had some sleep.'

'But I saw it, too,' Howard was saying, as Stanley shut the lab door after him.

I don't care what came through, Stanley said to himself. I don't care what you saw. I've done all I can. I haven't got anything left to give to this situation.

But *you* better have, Turpin, he realized. Because it's going to take a lot. What I've done disconnecting the augmented power source, getting the barrier erected, sending over the QB satellite, starting up the robot dredge — all that's nothing. Just a way of finding out what confronts us.

He thought, I wish I could sleep forever. Never wake up again and have to face this.

But he knew he had to.

And he was not the only one. They would all have to wake up, one by one, to face this, President Schwarz involved in his deft political maneuverings to outrun Jim Briskin, hitting him with his own idea . . . Briskin, too, because no matter what Schwarz had done, no matter how hurriedly and recklessly he had acted, the idea behind the colonization had been Briskin's. The responsibility remained essentially his, and Schwarz, now, would be quick to hand it back to him.

Having ascended to surface-level, Stanley passed through the wide front entrance of the TD building, down the steps and onto the morning sidewalk, the busy downtown Washington street of people and 'hoppers and jet'abs. The motion, the familiar, reassuring activity, made him feel better. This world, with its everyday sights, had not been blotted out, by any means; it remained solid, thoroughly substantial. As always.

He looked about for a jet'ab to take to his conapt.

Far off, at the corner of TD's administration building, a figure hurriedly disappeared.

Who was that? Don Stanley asked himself. He halted, forbore hailing the jet'ab. I know him, and I don't like him; it's somebody who in a day long past reminds me of things almost too repellent to recall, a part of my life that's dim, cut out, deliberately and for adequate reason forgotten. Mud, he thought. Yes, oddly enough, he thought. That man makes me think of mud and twisted plants, deranged organisms that burst poisonously and silently under a weak and utterly useless sun. Where is this? What have I been seeing?

What just happened now, a few minutes ago, back there on level one in TD's labs? He felt confused; standing on the sidewalk among the passing people he rubbed his forehead wearily, trying to rouse his mind. The swiftly-moving figure of course had been George Walt, but hadn't he — or rather they — closed down the Golden Door satellite and disappeared? He had heard that on TV or read it in the homeopapes. He was positive of it.

George Walt must be back, Stanley decided. From wherever they went.

Once more, a little dazedly, he began searching for a jet'ab to take him home.

13

AT THE BREAKFAST table in the small kitchen of his con-apt, Jim Briskin ate, and at the same time he carefully read the morning edition of the homeopape, finding in it, as a kind of minor melody in the momentous fugue which was playing itself out in heroic style, one item almost lost within the account of the migration of men and women to alter-Earth.

The first couple to cross over, Art and Rachael Chaffy, had been Cols. And the second couple, Stuart and Mrs. Hadley, had been white. It was exactly the sort of neat and tidy detail which appealed to Jim Briskin's sense of proportion, and he relaxed a little, enjoying his breakfast. Sal would be pleased by this, too, he realized. I'll have to remember to mention it to him when I see him later on this morning.

President Schwarz missed something, he reflected, by not noticing this minuscule fact at the time it was occurring. Schwarz could have made an extra-special superior speech to the two couples, presenting them with large gaudy plastic keys to the alternate universe, disclosing to them that they're a symbol of a new epic era in racial relations . . . as arranged for, of course, by the State's Rights Conservation Democratic Party in all its full and healthy glory. Some minion on Schwarz' staff slipped up, there, and should be fired.

He turned on the TV, then, to see if there was any later news. Had TD's engineering corps got the higher-yield power supply in operation yet, and if so, had the aperture been affected in the way anticipated? By now a lot more emigrants should have joined the Chaffys and the Hadleys there on the other side. He wondered if the Pithecanthropi-Sinanthropi people had taken notice already . . . had the crucial *Augenblick,* as the Germans put it, arrived by now? While he had slept?

On the TV screen the image gathered, became stable and fixed. But it was not what he had expected. The image had a certain grainy texture, familiar to him; it was emanating from a satellite which was still too far away. The sound, too, was distorted. It would, of course, clear up as the satellite moved closer, if it was moving in this direction and not away. What was going on? What was this peculiar program, anyhow? He leaned toward the speaker, trying to untangle the garble of words.

The video image became clarified, then. It was a head, the mutual head of the mutants George Walt. Its mouth opened and it spoke. 'I am king, now,' George Walt declared. 'I have at my disposal up here an entire army of what you'd like to think of as "near" men but which are actually — as you are about to find out and not from me — the legitimate tenants of this world and every other alternative Earth running parallel to us. You'd be surprised at the type of scientific discoveries which the Peking race — and I call them that merely as a means by which to identify them — have made over the centuries. They can, for instance, warp time and also space to suit their needs. They've tapped sources of energy unknown to you Homo sapiens. I have with me here in the Golden Door Moments of Bliss satellite the wisest and kindest philosopher from among their great people. Just a moment.' George Walt's head disappeared from the screen.

Merciful lord, Jim Briskin thought. He sat staring at the TV set, unable to take his eyes from it. George Walt are back, and they're out of their mind.

That's all we need, Jim said to himself. A crazy George Walt up there in their satellite, spinning around us. Now we've really got troubles.

His vidphone rang; automatically, he made his way over to answer it. 'Not just now,' he murmured. 'Call me later; I'm busy —'

'Don't hang up.' It was Tito Cravelli, sweating and agitated. 'I see you've got your TV set on. He . . . they have been broadcasting all morning, since about eight o'clock East Coast time. They're going to bring that Peke sage back on again; this is a video tape, it's running over and over again. Get a load of this so-called philosopher; you've never seen anything like it in your life. And then call me back.' Tito hung up.

Jim Briskin numbly returned to the TV set to listen and watch.

'I can walk through wood,' the TV set was saying, but it was not George Walt, now. It was as Tito had said, a Peking man, Sinanthropus telecasting from the Golden Door Moments of Bliss satellite. So George Walt . . . now you're in politics, Jim Briskin said to himself. And in a big way, too.

And we thought we were bad off before.

'Not only can I walk through wood,' the white-haired, massive-browed, enormous-chinned, ancient-looking Sinanthropus said, in reasonably good but somewhat mumbled English, 'but I can make myself invisible. The god of air empowers me wherever I go. He fills the sails of life with his magic breath, capable of accomplishing all things. Poor, puny Homo sapiens creatures! How could you conceivably expect to infest our world, with the Wind God himself present?'

By the Wind God, Jim Briskin realized with a sickened, enervating start, was meant George Walt.

He had never before quite thought of them that way, but there it was.

Let's see how President Schwarz decides to handle this, he said to himself. A Wind God in a satellite over our heads millions of fossil men straining to get at us. Darius Pethel can have his defective Jiffi-scuttler back; it's time we got rid of it, and by the quickest route possible. But how did this ancient Sinanthropus so-called philosopher get across to our world? Didn't anybody at TD notice his coming through?

They must have opened their own nexus, he decided. Either that or what he says is actually true; he *can* make himself invisible.

It was a gloomy prospect, having to wake up in the early morning and face this, to say the least.

And somebody has really lost this election now, he decided. Either Bill Schwarz or myself, depending on whom the electorate, in its understandable frenzy, decides to blame.

Going back to the kitchen table he seated himself and resumed eating his breakfast, now cold. As he mechanically ate, he pondered the chances of successfully shooting down the Golden Door satellite; surely that was the most likely next move for President Schwarz. After all, the exact position of the satellite at any given moment was known; it was — or had been until recently — printed on the entertainment page of every homeopape.

What I'm afraid of now, he realized, is that I'll look out the window of my decently private conapt and see Peking man walking along the sidewalk, and not just one but many of them.

He decided not to look, just to be on the safe side. At least not for a while. Instead he concentrated on finishing his breakfast, tasteless as it had become. As trivial a task as it was, at least it was a familiar event; it helped restore his sense of the regularity of reality.

Turning from the TV set Sal Heim released his emotion in an explosion of words. 'Call someone,' he said to his wife. 'Call Jim Briskin. Wait a minute; call Bill Schwarz at the White House — I'll talk to him direct myself. This is a national emergency; anybody with half an eye can see that. Party loyalty is out, you can wipe your nose on it. Let me know as soon as you have Bill Schwarz on the line.' He returned to watching the TV.

'Not only can I walk through wood and across the surface of water,' the great old Peking man on the screen was saying, 'But I can annihilate time.'

Good grief, Sal thought. This is awful. They can do all kinds of things we can't; they're centuries ahead of us. Who around here that I know can annihilate time? No one. He groaned aloud.

Pat said hecticly, 'I can't reach President Schwarz. The lines are tied up. Everybody must be . . .'

'Of course *they* are,' Sal said. 'The authorities know what this means. It's hopeless to try to get through to Schwarz. He'll have to get on the TV himself and tell the nation that a state of war exists between us and these dawn men. Or is this stuff on all channels?' Savagely, he turned the knob. The same image appeared on every other channel; the satellite was blanketing the airwaves. He was not surprised. I might have known, he said to himself with envenomed bitterness. Next we'll be picking them up on the vidphone.

'But more important than anything else,' the white-haired Peking man on the TV screen was saying, 'I can work exceeding wonderful, powerful magic. For I am a mighty magician; I can cause the stars to fall from the vault of the heavens and confusion to blind the eyes of all my foes. What do you respond to that, tiny Homo sapiens? You should have cogitated on that before you infested our world. *Facilis descensus Averno.* You see, through my use of supernatural forces, entirely unknown to your little race, I can speak in German.'

'Latin,' Sal murmured. 'You damn fool dawn man; that's Latin. So you don't know everything. Get off the TV so President Schwarz can declare war.' The image, however, remained.

Standing by his chair Patricia said, 'I guess this finishes Jim at the polls.'

'Didn't I just now get through saying that party doesn't count?' He glared at her; Pat shrank back. 'To cope with this we've got to think along entirely novel lines — everything is changed. I noticed one interesting thing. When George Walt were on they referred to us as "you Homo sapiens." Does that mean they're *not!* My god, you can't become a *converted* Sinanthropus; it's not like a church. I really have to talk to someone about this besides you,' he said scathingly to his wife. 'Someone who can come up with answers.'

Pat said, 'What about —'

'Wait,' He turned back to the TV screen. George Walt had once more appeared. 'They look older,' Sal said. 'I can't remember which of them is the artificial body. The one on right, as I recall. The real one has certainly done a good job of building it back, after we tore it to pieces.' He chuckled. 'We had them on the run, then. Our finest hour.' Once more he became grim. 'Too bad it's not like that now.'

'You know who I was going to suggest you call? Tito Cravelli. He always seems to be able to figure out what's happening.'

'Okay.' He nodded absently. 'Give me the phone; I'll call Tito.' He got to his feet, then. 'No, I'll get it myself. Why should you wait on me?' At the vidphone he paused and turned toward her. 'I'm sure it's the one on the right. You know, I'll bet at this moment everybody, including even Verne Engel and every last damn member of that rotten bunch CLEAN, would give his shirt if we could go back to, say, a month ago. To the way we were and the so-called "race problem" we had then. That's who I ought to call: Verne Engel. You know what I'd say to him? "You stupid bastard, does what you're fighting for look so real now? Skin pigment. What a laugh! Why not eye color? Too bad nobody ever thought of that. It cuts it a little finer, but basically it's the same thing. Okay, Verne, you get out there and die over the issue of upholding one certain eye color. Lots of luck."' Picking up the vidphone he dialed.

Pat said, 'What color eyes do Peking men have?'

Glaring at her Sal said, 'Christ, how would I know?'

'I just wondered. I never thought of it before.'

'Hello, Tito?' Sal said, as the vidscreen lighted. 'Get us out of this,' Sal said. 'Find where they're getting through into our world and plug it up, an then we'll figure out how to knock down the Golden Door Moments of Bliss satellite. You agree? Tito, say something.'

'I know where they're getting through,' Tito said, laconically.

Sal turned to his wife. 'You were right. He does know.' He turned back to the vidscreen. 'Well, what do we do? How do we . . .'

'We make a deal,' Tito Cravelli said in a harsh, totally dry voice.

Staring at him Sal said, 'We what? I don't believe it.'

'And we'll be lucky if we can manage that,' Tito added. 'There are a few things you don't know, Sal. This attack on us by the Pekes is coming out of a hundred years in the future. George Walt have had an entire century to work with them, filling in the gaps in their culture, teaching them as many of our techniques as they could cram into them in that time . . . and it's a very long time. Don't ask me how I found this out; just take my word that it's the case. The nexus that they're using is at TD, but we can't close it; they're supplying it with power from the other side, a possibility which doesn't seem to have occurred to anyone at TD until it was too late. In other words, until now.'

'What *kind* of deal?'

'I don't know yet. I'm seeing Jim Briskin in a few moments; we're going to try to think of something we can offer them — offer George Walt actually, since they're doing the talking. As I see it, the Pekes don't actually need to expand into our world; they haven't even filled up their own. They have no pressing population problem, as we have. So there may be something they want and can use more than mere land. Because that's all they're going to find if they try to come over here. I know damn well our people will put up a fight until there's nothing left standing. It'll be a scorched-earth planet . . . we can promise them that. As a starter.'

Turning to Pat, Sal said, 'We're going to make a deal; there's no other way out.'

'I heard,' she said. 'I wish I hadn't; I didn't want to hear that.'

'Isn't that something? Our ancestors didn't make a deal. They wiped the Pekes out.'

'But now,' Pat said, 'they have George Walt.'

He nodded. Evidently that made the difference. But he had a terrible feeling that Tito Cravelli was wrong as to the quantity of techniques that George Walt had passed on to the Pekes. His intuition was that the transfer of knowledge had gone the other way: it had been the Pekes who had educated George Walt.

Jim Briskin said half-ironically, 'We can offer them the *Encyclopedia Britannica,* translated into their language.' If they have a written language, he added to himself. Or if George Walt haven't given them that already. 'Maybe George Walt have passed them everything they'll ever need,' he said to Tito Cravelli, who sat moodily facing him across the room. 'I'd assume that during the next century George Walt probably have gone back and forth continually.' He could picture it, and it was not encouraging.

'Who can we ask for help from?' Sal Heim said, to no one in particular. 'Call God.' His wife patted his arm, sympathetically. 'Don't do that,' Sal complained. 'It distracts me. In the name of something-or-other there must be *somebody* we can turn to.'

The vidphone rang and Tito Cravelli rose to answer it. After a few moments he returned. 'That was my contact at TD. At this moment, while we're sitting here muttering pointless maledictions, Pekes are pouring through the rent.'

Everyone in the room stared at him.

'That's right,' Tito said, nodding. 'So already now the TD administration building is full of them; in fact they're beginning to leak out into downtown Washington, D.C. Leon Turpin's been conversing with President Schwarz, but so far . . .' He shrugged. 'They erected a concrete barrier in front of the rent but the Pekes simply moved the rent to one side. And kept on coming across.' He added, 'Bohegian, my contact, is leaving the TD building; they're being evacuated.'

'Christ,' Sal Heim said. 'Christ, sweet shimmering Christ.'

Pat Heim said, 'You know who I'd like to see you talk to?' She glanced around at the others. 'Bill Smith.'

'Who's that?' Cravelli asked sharply. 'Oh yeah. The Peke. That anthropologist Dillingsworth has him. What could Bill Smith tell us?'

'He would know what they lack,' Patricia said. 'Maybe for instance they've been trying for a dozen centuries to achieve a space drive. We could turn a small rocket engine over to them, one with only a million pounds of thrust or so. Or maybe they don't have music. Think what it would mean: We could start them out with single instruments such as the harmonica or the Jew's harp or the electric guitar . . .'

'Yes,' Cravelli agreed acidly, 'But George Walt have already done that. At least, we've got to assume that. You heard that Peke talking Latin; I didn't grasp, really genuinely grasp, how much George Walt have accomplished until I heard that . . . then I threw in the sponge. I don't mind admitting it; that's when I gave up, pure and simple.'

'And decided to plead for a deal,' Sal Heim said, half to himself.

'That's right,' Cravelli said. 'Then I knew we had to come to some kind of terms. It didn't terrify you to hear Sinanthropus talking Latin? It should have.'

'I've got it,' Pat Heim said. 'That one Sinanthropus, that old white-haired so-called philosopher up in the satellite, he's a mutant. More evolved than the others, greater cranial area or something, especially in the forehead region. Unique. George Walt are pulling the wool over our eyes.'

'But they are pouring through the nexus rent,' Cravelli said coldly. 'Whether they speak Latin or don't. If Leon Turpin has ordered the TD administration building evacuated, you know it's critical.'

'I've got it,' Pat said, 'Oh my god, I've really got it. Listen to me. Let's turn the Smithsonian Institute over to the Pekes in exchange for them leaving. What about that?'

'Institution,' Cravelli said, correcting her.

'And if that's not enough,' Pat said, 'we'll throw in the Library of Congress. They'd be smart to take that. What an offer!'

'You know,' Sal said, hunching forward and gazing steadily down at his knees, 'she may have something there. Look what they'd get out of that; the entire assembled, collected artifacts and knowledge of our culture. A hell of a lot more — incredibly much more — than George Walt can give them. It's the wisdom of four thousand years. Boy, I tell you; I'd take it in a second if it were offered to me.'

After a long pause Tito Cravelli said, 'But we're forgetting something. None of us are in a position to make the Pekes any kind of offer; none of us hold any official position in the government. Now, if you were already in office, Jim . . .'

'Take it to Schwarz,' Sal said.

'We'd have to,' Pat agreed rapidly. 'And that means going to the White House, since the phone lines are all tied up. Which one of us would Schwarz be willing to see? Assuming he'd see any of us.'

Sal said, 'It would have to be Jim.'

Shrugging, Jim Briskin said, 'I'll go. It's better than merely sitting around here talking.' It all seemed futile to him anyhow. But at least this way he'd be doing something.

'Who're you going to take the offer to ultimately?' Cravelli asked him. 'Bill Smith?'

'No,' Jim said. 'To that white-haired Sinanthropic philosopher up in the satellite.' Obviously, he was the one to go to; he held the power.

'George Walt aren't going to like it when they hear it,' Cravelli pointed out. 'You'll have to talk fast; they'll do their best to shut you up.'

'I know,' Jim said, rising to his feet and moving toward the door. 'I'll phone you from Washington and let you know how I made out.'

As he left the apartment, he heard Sal saying, 'I think, though, we ought to take the *Spirit of St Louis* out when the Pekes aren't looking and keep it. They won't know it's gone; what do they know about airplanes?'

'And the Wright brothers' plane,' Pat said, as he started to shut the door after him. He paused, then, as he heard her 'Do you think he'll get in to see President Schwarz?'

'Not a chance,' Sal said emphatically. 'But what else can we do? It's the best we could come up with on such short notice.'

'He'll get in,' Cravelli disagreed. 'I'll make you a dime bet.'

'You know what else we could have offered?' Pat said. 'The Washington Monument.'

'What the hell would the Pekes do with that?' Sal demanded.

Jim shut the door after him and walked down the corridor to the elevator. None of them, he reflected, had offered to come with him. But what difference did it make? There was nothing they could do vis-a-vis President Schwarz . . . and perhaps nothing he could do, either. And even if he did get in to see Schwarz, and even if Schwarz went along with the idea — how far did that carry him? What were the chances that he could sell the Sinanthropic philosopher on the idea with George Walt present?

But I'm still going to try it, he decided. Because the alternative, a general war, would doom our colonists there on the other side; it's their lives we're trying to save.

And anyhow, he realized, none of us wants to start slaughtering the Peking people. It would be too much like the old days, back among our cave-dwelling ancestors. Back to their level. We must have grown out of that by now, he said to himself. And if we haven't — what does it matter who wins?

Four hours later, from a public vidphone booth in downtown Washington, D.C, Jim Briskin called back to report He felt bone-weary and more than a little depressed, but at least the first hurdle had been jumped successfully.

'So he liked the idea,' Tito Cravelli said.

Jim said, 'Schwarz is madly grasping at any straw he can find, and there aren't even very many of them. Everyone in Washington is prepared to shoot down the Golden Door Moments of Bliss satellite, of course; they'll do that if my attempt at negotiation fails, my attempt to split George Walt off from the Pekes.'

'If we shoot down the satellite,' Cravelli said, 'then we'd have to fight to the bitter death. Either our race or theirs would be wiped out, and we can't have that, not in this day and age. With the weapons we've got and what they possibly have . . .'

'Schwarz realizes that. He appreciates all the nuances of the situation. But he can't just sit idle while Pekes pour across at will. We're walking a highly tricky line. It's not in our interest to make this into a full-scale hydrogen bomb war, and yet we don't want simply to capitulate. Schwarz says to go ahead with the Smithsonian, but to hold back on the Library of Congress as long as possible, to give it up only under the greatest pressure. I tend to agree.' He added, 'They're sending me up there; I'll do it myself.'

'Why you? What's the matter with the State Department? Don't they have anyone who can do that sort of work any more?'

'I asked to go.'

'You're nuts. George Walt hates you already.'

'Yes,' Jim agreed, 'but I think I know how to handle this; I've got an idea of how I can impair the relationship between George Walt and the Pekes in such a way that it can't be repaired. Anyhow, it's worth a try.'

'Don't tell me what your idea is,' Cravelli said. 'Tell me after it works. If it doesn't work, don't tell me at all.'

Jim grinned starkly. 'You're a hard man. You might be too ruthless as Attorney General; I'll have to rethink that, possibly.'

'It's signed and sealed,' Cravelli said. 'You can't get out of it. Good luck up on the satellite.' He rang off, then.

Leaving the phone booth, Jim Briskin walked along the half-deserted sidewalk until he came to a parked, empty jet-hopper.

'Take me to the Golden Door satellite,' he said, opening the door and getting in.

'The Golden Door is closed down,' the 'hopper driver said languidly. 'No more girls up there. Just some goof broadcasting that he's king of the world or some crazy thing like that.' He turned to face Jim. 'However, I know a gnuvvy doggone place in the north west side of town that I can . . .'

'The satellite,' Jim said. 'Okay? Just drive the 'hopper and let me decide where I want to go.'

'You Cols,' the driver muttered as he started the 'hopper up. 'You sure always got a chip on your shoulder. All right, buddy, have it your way. But you're going to be disappointed when you get up there.'

Silently, Jim leaned back against the seat and sat waiting as the 'hopper rose into the sky.

At the landing field on the satellite, George Walt personally met him, hand outstretched. 'This is George,' the head said, as Jim shook hands with whichever of them it was. 'I knew they'd want to talk terms, but I didn't expect them to send you, Briskin.'

'This is Walt,' the head said then, belligerently. 'I certainly have no desire to do business with you, Briskin. Go back and tell them . . . ' The mouth struggled as both brothers sought to make use of it simultaneously.

'What does it matter who they send?' the head — no doubt George, now — said at last. 'Come below to the office, Briskin, where we can make ourselves comfortable. I have a hunch this darn business might take quite a while.'

It was extraordinary how much George Walt had aged. They had a wrinkled, brittle, almost frail quality about them, and when they walked they moved slowly, hesitantly, as if afraid of falling, as if they were terribly infirm. What would account for this? Jim wondered. And then he understood. George Walt were now *jerries*. One hundred years had passed for them since he had last seen them. He wondered how much longer they could keep going. Certainly not for too great a period. But their mental energies were undimmed. He could still sense the enor-

mous alertness emanating from them; they remained as formidable as ever.

In George Walt's office sat the huge, white-haired old Sinanthropus; he watched warily from beneath his beetling brows
as Jim Briskin entered, obviously suspicious at once. It would
be no easy task, Jim realized, to come to terms with this man.
Mistrust was profoundly written on his massive-jawed, sloping
face.

'We've got them where we want them,' George Walt said ex-
pansively to the Sinanthropus. 'This man's coming up here —
Jim Briskin is his name — verifies it.' Both eyes flamed with
gloating.

In a hoarse voice, the Sinanthropus said, 'What will you offer
us if we abandon your world?'

Jim Briskin said, 'That which we prize beyond everything
else. Our most valued possession.'

The Sinanthropus and George Walt watched him fixedly.

'The Smithsonian Institution in Washington, D.C.,' Jim said.

'Wait a minute' / 'We're not interested in that!' George Walt
said together. 'That won't do; that's out of the question. We
want political and economic priority over the North American
land mass — otherwise the invasion continues. What kind of offer is the Smithsonian? That's nothing but a museum.' / 'Who
wants a museum? This is ridiculous!' Both eyes blazed with
outraged and uneasy anger.

The Sinanthropus, however, said slowly and distinctly, 'I am
reading Mr Briskin's mind, and I am interested. Please be silent.
Wind God, it goes without saying that your opinion is valuable,
but it is I who must make the actual decision.'

'The conference is over!' / 'I've heard enough,' George Walt
said. 'Go back below to Terra, Briskin; you're not wanted here.' /
'Let's call this off.'

'There is, in the back of your mind,' the Sinanthropus said to

Jim, 'the thought that you will, if pressed, add in the Library of Congress. I will consider that offer as well.'

'We'd prefer not to add that,' Jim said, 'but if we have to, we have to.' He felt resigned.

'Goodbye, Briskin,' George Walt said. 'See you some time. It's evident that you're trying to make a side deal, here, trying to cut my brother and me out. But we won't be cut out.' The head added emphatically, 'I agree. You're completely wasting your time, Briskin.' One of George Walt's four arms was extended, then, 'Until next time.'

'Until next time,' Jim said, shaking hands. Taking a deep, unsteady breath he all at once yanked with every dyne of strength which he could muster; the hand and arm came loose from the artificial body and he was left holding them.

Bewildered, the Sinanthropus said, 'Wind God, it seems strange to me that your arm is detachable.'

'This is no Wind God,' Jim Briskin said. 'You've been misled. Our people were, too, for a good long time. This is an ordinary man with an extra, artificial body.' He pointed to the wiring visible within the gaping shoulder.

'A Homo sapiens, you mean?' the stooped old Sinanthropus said. 'Like yourself?' Slow but exact comprehension began to form in his reddish eyes.

'Not only is he not a Wind God,' Jim said, 'but he's been for decades the owner of a . . . I dislike naming it outright.'

'Name it!'

'Let's simply call it a house of pleasure. He's a businessman. No more, no less.'

'I can think of nothing more obnoxious to the mores of my people,' the Sinanthropus said to George Walt, 'than a hoax of this stripe. You swore to us that you were our Wind God. And in fulfillment of many myths, your unusual anatomy seemed to prove it.' He panted slowly, raggedly.

'"Unusual"', George Walt echoed. 'You mean unique. In all of the parallel Earths — and God knows exactly how many there may be — you won't find anyone, anyone at all, like me.' He amended quickly, 'Like us, rather. And consider this satellite. What do you think keeps it up? The wind, of course; how else could it stay up here, month after month? Obviously I control the wind, as I told you. Otherwise this satellite would . . .'

'I could destroy you,' the old Sinanthropus said. He no longer seemed much impressed by George Walt's line of argument. 'But I am frankly too disappointed to care one way or another. It's clear to me, and I will soon see that it's equally clear to my people, that you Homo sapiens are a treacherous lot. Probably best avoided,' To Jim he said, 'Is that so?'

'We're known for that,' Jim agreed.

'And that's how you triumphed originally over our ancestors on this parallel world?'

'You're damn right,' Jim said. He added, 'And we'd do it again, given half a chance.'

'Probably you would not genuinely have delivered that museum of yours to us,' the Sinanthropus said, 'the name of which I have already forgotten. Well, no matter. Obviously it's impossible to do business with you Homo sapiens; you're adept, polished liars. Nothing we agreed on would remain truly binding in such a milieu. My people lack even a name for such conduct.'

'No wonder we had so little trouble wiping you out,' Jim said.

'In view of your dedication to fraud,' the Sinanthropus said, 'I see no real point in my remaining here; the longer I go on, the more immersed I become. Personally, I regret this whole encounter; my people have suffered by it already. God knows what would become of us if we were so naive as to try to continue.' An unhappy expression on his face, the aged, white-haired Sinanthropus turned his back and walked away from Jim Briskin and George Walt. 'It would be unnatural for people of our race to seek to participate in an exclusively destructive relationship,' he said, over his shoulder. And vanished. One moment he stood there, the next he had gone. Even George Walt seemed taken aback; both eyes blinked. The Sinanthropus, by means of his so called magic, had returned to his own world.

'Smart,' George Walt said, presently. 'You handled that extremely well, Briskin. I never saw it coming. One hundred years of work gone down the drain. Give me my arm back and we'll call it quits; I'm too old to go through this kind of thing any more.' The head added, 'You're probably right After all, politically speaking, Briskin is a professional; he can run rings around us. What happened here just now demonstrates that.'

'Honesty generally wins out,' Jim said.

'You call that trash you peddled to that half-animal just now — you call that *honesty*? *I* never heard such a mass of twisted . . .' George Walt broke off, then. 'Like everybody else. I more or less trusted you, Briskin. It never occurred to me you'd trade on such techniques to win an issue. Your integrity's just a myth! Probably dreamed up by your campaign manager.'

'You mean you actually are their Wind God?'

'Pragmatically speaking, yes. Every one of us, in relation to them, are gods . . . speaking in terms of the evolutionary hierarchy, anyhow, in the broadest possible sense.'

Jim said, 'Was it you who enabled them to shoot apart the QB observation satellite?'

Nodding, George Walt said, 'Yes, it was. By my magic.'

'What you mean,' Jim said, 'is that you ferried a ground-to-air guided missile over to them. Magic, my foot.' He looked at his wristwatch. 'I have to get back down to Earth; I've got a major speech to record. You care to accompany me back to my 'hopper?'

'I'm busy,' George Walt said curtly. 'I have to fit my arm back on. This whole business makes me sick, and not only that, terribly angry; I'm going to initiate beamed broadcasts twenty-four hours a day on all frequencies denouncing you, as soon as I can get the satellite's transmitter started up again. I look forward to your losing in November, Briskin; that's the one nice thing I can count on.'

'Suit yourself,' Jim said, shrugging. He left the office, made his way to the elevator. Behind him, George Walt brought a tool kit out from their desk and began the task of repairing the damage to the artificial body which Jim Briskin had purposefully accomplished. The expression on George Walt's face was one of great gloom.

In his entrenched position, along with other company personnel, on the outskirts of the flank of the TD administration building in Washington, D.C., Don Stanley noted all at once, and to his complete surprise, a sudden lull in the fierce racket from the Pekes within.

'Some darn thing has happened,' Howard conjectured, also aware of the unexpected silence. 'We better get set for another rush; they're probably determined to overwhelm us this time. Before that idiot Schwarz can get army . . .'

'Wait,' Stanley said, listening. 'You know what I think? I think the fliegemer Pekes are gone.'

Puzzled, Howard said, 'Gone where?'

Rising to his haunches Stanley peered at the administration building, at the shattered windows on the nearest side, and the conviction came to him stronger than ever that the building was now, for some totally obscure and merciful reason, deserted. With caution, aware of the acute risk he was taking, he began to walk slowly step by step toward the front entrance.

'They'll pop you out of existence,' Howard called to him warningly, 'with those funny little weapons of theirs; better get back down, you half-wit.' But he, too, stood up. So did a number of armed company police.

Opening the familiar front door of the building, Stanley peeped inside.

He saw no sign of Pekes anywhere. The halls were empty and silent. The invasion by the chinless dawn men from the parallel Earth had ceased as abruptly as it had begun, and somewhat more mysteriously.

Howard, joining him, said, 'Um, we scared them off.'

'Scared them off nothing. They changed their collective minds.' Stanley started in the direction of the elevator leading to the floor one subsurface labs. 'I have an intuition,' he said over his shoulder to Howard. 'And I want to verify it as soon as I can.'

When he and Howard reached the labs, Stanley discovered that he was right... and a good thing, too. The nexus joining the two parallel Earths had vanished.

'They ... closed it down,' Howard said, wonderingly craning his neck, as if expecting to see it crop up once more in a remote corner.

'So now,' Stanley murmured, 'our problem is to reopen our own earlier nexus. The original one. And make the try to relocate our colonists before the moment in which they're wiped out.' The chances of success struck him as being not very good, and yet of course the attempt had to be made.

'Why do you think they called their invasion off?' Howard asked.

Stanley gestured emptily. 'Maybe they didn't like it here after all.' Who knew? Certainly he did not. Perhaps they would never know. In any case they had their work cut out for them; several thousand men and women on the other side were wholly dependent on them for their lives. For their safe return to this world. Remembering the human skeletons which had been dredged up from the swamp a hundred years hence. Stanley felt deep forebodings. At best we can only save some of them, he realized. But that's better than nothing. Even if we save only *one* life, it's worth it.

'How long do you think it'll take to make contact with our people stranded over there?' Howard asked him. 'A day? As long as a week?'

'Let's find out,' Stanley said shortly, and started at once in the direction of the power supply of Dar Pethel's defective Jiffi-scuttler.

The depressing task of bringing the colonists back from alter-Earth had begun.

14

IN NOVEMBER, DESPITE the abusive broadcasts from the Golden Door Moments of Bliss satellite, or because of them, Jim Briskin succeeded in nosing out the incumbent Bill Schwarz and thereby won the presidential election.

So now, at long last, Salisbury Heim said to himself, we have a Negro President of the United States. A new epoch in human understanding has arrived.

At least, let's hope so.

'What we need,' Patricia said meditatively, 'is a party, so we can celebrate.'

'I'm too tired to celebrate,' Sal said. It had been a tough haul from the nominating convention to this; he remembered clearly every inch of it. The worst part, it went without saying, had been the collapse of the abortive emigration program announced in Jim's Chicago speech; why that had not put a permanent end to Jim's election chances, Sal Heim did not know even at this late date. Perhaps it was because Bill Schwarz had managed to move so adroitly, had embroiled himself — deliberately — in the situation; hence much, if not most, of the ultimate blame had fallen on him, not on Jim.

'But we deserve to take a little time off to relax,' Pat pointed out. 'We've been working for months; if we go on this way ...'

'One beer at one small bar,' Sal decided. 'And then bed? I'll compromise at that.' He did not especially enjoy going out in public, these days; inevitably he rubbed up against some individual who had been a part of the colonizing effort on alter-Earth or who, anyhow, had a brother-in-law who had gone trustingly over there. Such encounters had been rather unpleasant; he always found himself trying to answer questions which simply could not be answered. *Why'd you get us into that?* had been the *primary* inquiry, asked in a variety of ways, but still always amounting to the same thing. And yet, despite this, they had won.

'I think we should get together with a few people,' Pat disagreed. 'Certainly with Jim; that goes without saying. And then Leon Turpin, if he'll join us, because after all it was Mr Turpin who got us off the hook by bringing those people back to our world — or anyhow his engineers did. *Someone* at TD did. It was TD that saved us, Sal; let's finally face it and give credit where credit is due.'

'All right,' Sal said. 'Just so long as that little Kansas City businessman who showed up with that defective 'scuttler isn't along; that's all I insist on.' The man on account of whom all the trouble had broken out in the first place. At the moment, Sal could not even recall his name, an obvious Freudian block.

'The one I blame,' Pat said, 'is Lurton Sands.'

'Then don't invite him either,' Sal said. But there was hardly much chance of that; Sands was in prison, right now, for his crime against the sleeping bibs and his ridiculous attempt on Jim's life. As was Cally Vale for having lasered the 'scuttler repairman. That whole business had been excessively melancholy, both intrinsically and as a conspicuous harbinger of the difficulties which it had ushered into their collective lives, difficulties which by no means were over.

'You know,' Pat said fretfully, 'there's one thing that still, right now, I can't quite get out of my mind. I keep having this sneaking, nervous anxiety that. . . .' She smiled at him uneasily, her jessamine lips twitching. 'I hope I don't pass it on to you, but . . .'

'But deep down inside,' Sal finished for her, 'you're afraid a few of those Pekes have stayed on this side.'

'Yes.' She nodded.

Sal said, 'I get the same damn intimation, now and then. Late at night, I keep looking out of the corner of my eye, especially on the street when I see someone furtive looking hurrying away around a corner to get out of sight And the funny thing is that from what Jim tells me, I know he feels exactly the same way. Maybe we all have a residual sense of guilt connected with the Pekes . . . after all, we did invade their world first. It's our consciences bothering us.'

Shivering, as she was wearing only a weightless Tafek-web negligee, his wife said, 'I hope that's all it is. Because I'd really hate to run into a Peke some dark night; I'd think right away that they'd opened a nexus again into our world at some point and were very carefully, secretly, ferrying a wide stream of their cousins and aunts across.'

As if we're not desperately overcrowded as it is, Sal thought, without having to cope with *that* any more.

'What I can never comprehend,' he murmured, 'is why they didn't accept our liberal offer of the Smithsonian. And for that matter the Library of Congress. Gosh, they pulled out without getting anything.'

'Pride,' Pat said.

'No.' Sal shook his head.

'Stupidity, then. Dumb, dawn-man stupidity. There's no frontal lobe inside that sloping forehead.'

'Maybe.' He shrugged. 'But how can you expect one species to follow the logic of another? They operate at their level; we operate at ours. And never the twain will meet . . . I hope.' Anyhow not in his lifetime, he said to himself. Maybe a later generation will be open-minded enough to accept such things, but not now; not we who inhabit this world at this particular moment.

'Shall I ask Mr Turpin to come here to our place?' Pat asked. 'Are we going to have the party here?'

'Maybe Turpin won't want to celebrate Jim's victory,' Sal said. 'He and Schwarz were pretty thick through most of the campaign.'

'Let me ask you something,' Pat said suddenly. 'Do you think George Walt really are a Wind God? After all, they were born with two bodies and four arms and legs, the artificial part wasn't installed until much later. So originally they were exactly what they pretended to be. Jim didn't tell that Sinanthropus that.'

'You're darn right he didn't,' Sal said vigorously. 'And don't you rock the boat out of any misplaced ethical motives . . . you hear?'

'Okay,' she said, nodding.

Outside on the sidewalk a gang of well-wishers yelled up praise and slogans of congratulations; the racket filtered into the conapt, and Sal went to glance out the living room window.

Some Cols, he saw. And also some Whites. Just what he hoped to see; just what the entire struggle had been about. How long it had been in coming . . . almost two centuries more than it should have taken. The mind of man was uncommonly stubborn and slow to change. Reformers, including himself, were always prone to forget that. Victory always seemed just around the corner. But generally it was not, after all.

A vote for Jim Briskin, he thought, recalling the clichés and tirades of the campaign, *is a vote for humanity itself.* Stale now, and always oversimplified, and yet deep underneath substantially true. The slogan had embodied the motor which had driven them on, which had, finally, enabled them to win. And now what? Sal asked himself. The big problems, every one of them, still remained. The bibs, in their all too many warehouses throughout the nation, had become the property of Jim Briskin and the Republican-Liberal Party. As had the desolate, roving packs of unemployed Cols, not to mention the unhappy lower fringes of the white in-group . . . men such as Mr Hadley, who had been the first White to emigrate, as well as nearly the first to come stumbling back, after the nexus had, mercifully, been reopened.

It'll be a hard four years for Jim, he realized soberly. He's inherited a vast, savage burden from Schwarz. If he thinks he's worn down now, he should see himself next year or the year after that. But I guess that's what he wants. I hope so, anyhow.

Did we get or learn *anything* from our unexpected confrontation with the Pekes? he wondered.

It showed us, he decided, that the difference between say myself and the average Negro is so damn slight, by every truly meaningful criterion, that for all intents and purposes it doesn't exist. When something like that, a contact with a race that's not Homo sapiens, occurs, at last we can finally see this. And I don't mean just myself; it was given to me to see this from the start. I mean the ordinary (statistically speaking) fat, mean slob who plops down next to you on a jet-hopper, snatches up a homeo-pape that someone's left, reads a headline, and then begins to spout right and left his miserable opinions. So maybe, in the final analysis, this is what won the election for Jim. Could it be? Admittedly, we can never be certain. But we can make an educated guess and say yes, maybe so. Maybe it was.

In that case, the whole wretched fracas was worth while.

'All the time you've been standing there in your dreams of self-glory,' Pat said archly, 'I've been on the vid getting hold of people for our party. Mr Turpin can't come or doesn't care to come, which is more likely, but he's sending a few of his carefully cultivated big-time employees — an administrative assistant named Donald Stanley, for instance, whom he said we ought to meet. He didn't say why.'

'I know why,' Sal said. 'Tito Cravelli mentioned him, and anyhow I met him personally on our trip to alter-Earth. Stanley was directly in charge of the defective 'scuttler and, in a sense, was responsible for getting the entire project going. Yes, Stanley certainly should be part of this get-together. And I hope you called Tito. Our man in the world.'

'I'll call him now,' Pat said, 'and can you think of anyone else?'

'The more the better,' Sal said, beginning finally to get into the spirit of the thing.

Late at night Darius Pethel worked alone in his closed-up store. Something tapped on the window, and he glanced up, startled. There, on the dark sidewalk, stood Stuart Hadley.

Going to the front door, Pethel unlocked it. Opening it he said, 'I thought you emigrated.'

'Cut it out. You know we all came back.' Shoulders hunched, Hadley entered the store. The familiar place where he had worked so long.

'How was it over there?'

'Awful.'

'So I heard,' Pethel said. 'I suppose you want your job back. With each and every trimming.'

'Why not? I'm as good as I ever was.' Restlessly, Hadley roamed about the marginal shadowy spaces of the store. 'You'll be glad to hear I'm back with my wife. Sparky returned to the Golden Door satellite; they're going to open it again. In spite of Jim Briskin's election. I guess there's going to be a showdown fight.' He added, 'Frankly I couldn't care less. I've got my own problems. Well? What do you say? Can I come back?' He tried to make it sound casual.

'No reason why not,' Pethel said.

'Thanks.' Hadley looked relieved. Very much so.

'Some of you fellas got killed, I read. Nasty.'

'That's right, Dar; you've got it. They attacked us and the U.S. military unit accompanying us fought them off bang-upwise until the entrance, or maybe I should say exit, was reopened. I'd rather not talk about it, to tell you the truth. So many verflugender hopes went down the drainpipe when that failed, mine and a lot of other people's. Now it's all up to the new president; we'll wait, bide our time, see what he can dream up, I guess. That's about all we can do, whether we like it or not.'

'You can write letters to homeopapes.'

Hadley glared at him in mute outrage. 'Some joke. You're personally okay, Dar; you're all set. But what about the rest of us? Briskin better come up with something, or it's going to get a lot worse before it gets better.'

'How do you like knowing you're going to have a Col for president?'

'I voted for him, along with the others.' Hadley wandered back to the locked front door of the store. 'Can I start tomorrow?'

'Sure. Come in at nine.'

'You think life is worth living, Dar?' Hadley demanded suddenly.

'Who knows. And if you have to ask, there's something wrong with you. What's the matter, are you sick or something? I'm not hiring anybody who's a nut or mentally flammy; you better get straightened out before you show up here tomorrow morning.'

'The compassionate employers.' Hadley shook his head, 'Sorry I asked. I should have known better.'

'That emigration stunt with that This-Olt girl didn't apparently teach you anything; you're as fouled up as ever, What's the matter, can't you accept life as it is? You've always got to pine after what isn't? A hell of a lot of men would envy you your job; you're incredibly darn lucky to get it back.'

'I know that.'

'Then why don't you calm down? What's the matter?'

'When you had hopes once,' Hadley explained after a pause, 'it's always hard to go on after you give them up. It's not so hard to give them up; *that* part is easy. After all, you've got to, sometimes. But afterward . . .' He gestured, grunting, '. . . What takes their place? Nothing. And the emptiness is frightening. It's so big. It sort of absorbs everything else; sometimes it's bigger than the whole world. It grows. It becomes bottomless. Do you know what I'm talking about?'

'No,' Pethel said. Nor did he particularly care.

'You're lucky. Maybe it'll never hit you, or anyhow not until old age, until you're a hundred and fifty or so.' Hadley gazed at him. 'I envy you.'

'Take a pill,' Pethel said.

'I'd be glad to take a pill, if I knew of one. I don't think they'd help, though. I feel like taking a long walk: maybe I'll walk all night. You give a darn? Do you want to come along? Hell no, you don't. I can see that.'

Pethel said, 'I've got work to do; I don't have time to stroll around taking in the sights. I tell you what, Hadley. When you come back to work tomorrow — listen to this — I'll give you a raise. Does that cheer you up?' He peered at him, trying to see.

'Yes,' Hadley said, but without conviction.

'I thought it would.'

'Maybe Briskin will go back to advocating planet-wetting.'

'Would that interest you? That tired old nothing program?'

Opening the door, Hadley moved back outside into the dark sidewalk. 'Anything would interest me. To be honest. I'd buy anything, right now.'

Gloomily, knowing that he had failed somewhere in this interchange with Hadley, Darius Pethel said, 'Some employee you're going to make.'

'I can't help it,' Hadley pointed out. 'Maybe I'll change, though, in time; maybe something'll come along. God, I'm still hoping!' He seemed amazed, even a little disgusted with himself.

'You know what you could try for a change?' Pethel said. 'Showing up a little early, a few minutes *before* nine. It might alter your life. Even more than that moronic attempt to escape by sneaking off with that girl to that weird world where those semi-apes live. Try it. See if I'm not right.'

Hadley eyed him. 'You mean it. And that's the whole point; that's why we don't understand each other. Maybe I should feel sorry for you instead of trying to get you to feel sorry for me. You know, maybe someday you'll suddenly crack up completely, fly into a million pieces without warning. And I'll limp on for years. Never really give up, never actually stop. Interesting.'

'For a person who used to be optimistic . . .'

'I've aged,' Hadley said briefly. 'That experience on that alter-world did it to me. Can't you see it in my face?' He nodded goodbye to Darius Pethel, then. 'See you tomorrow. Bright and early.'

As he shut the door, Pethel said to himself, I hope he can still peddle 'scuttlers. We'll see about that. If not, he's out. For good. As far as I'm concerned, he's just back here on probation, and he's lucky to get *that*.

He's sure depressing to talk to these days, Pethel said to himself as he returned to his back office.

That raise in salary will eventually cheer him up, he decided. How can it not?

His own meager tendency to doubt was assuaged by that timely realization. Thoroughly. Or . . . was it? Down underneath on a level which he did not care to communicate, a region of his mind which remained his own damn business, he was not so sure.

His feet up on the arm of the couch, Phil Danville said, 'It was my majestic speeches that did it for you, Jim. So what's my reward?' He grinned. 'I'm waiting.' He waited. 'Well?'

'Nothing on Earth could ever be sufficient reward for such an accomplishment,' Jim Briskin said absently.

'He's got his mind on something else,' Danville said, appealing to Dorothy Gill. 'Look at him. He's not even happy; he's going to ruin Sal Heim's party, when we get there. Maybe we better not go.'

'We have to go,' Dorothy Gill said.

'I won't wreck the mood of the party,' Jim assured them, drawing himself up dutifully. 'I'll be over it by the time we get there.' After all, this was *the* moment. But actually the great historic instant had already managed to slide away and disappear; it was too elusive, too subtly interwoven into the texture of more commonplace reality. And, in addition, the problems awaiting him seemed to efface his recognition of anything else. But that was the way it had to be.

The door of the room opened and a Peke entered, carrying a portable version of a TD linguistics machine. At the sight of him everyone jumped to their feet. The three Secret servicemen whipped out their guns and one of them yelled, 'Drop!' The people in the room sprawled clumsily, dropping to the floor in grotesque, inexpert heaps, scrambling without dignity away from the line of prospective fire.

'Hello, Homo friends,' the Peke said, by means of the linguistics machine. 'I wish in particular to thank you, Mr Briskin, for permitting me to remain in your world. I will comport myself entirely within the framework of your legal code, believe me. And, in addition, perhaps later ...'

The three Secret servicemen put their laser pistols away and slowly returned to their inobtrusive places about the room.

'Good lord,' Dorothy Gill breathed in relief as she got unsteadily to her feet. 'It's only Bill Smith. This time, anyhow.' She sank back down in her chair, sighing. 'We're safe for a little while longer.'

'You really gave us a scare,' Jim Briskin said to the Peke, He found himself still shaking. 'I don't remember having had anything to do with permitting him to stay here,' he said to Tito Cravelli.

'He's thanking you in advance,' Tito said. 'You're going to decide after you become president, or rather he hopes so.'

Phil Danville said, 'Let's take him along with us to the party. That ought to please Sal Heim. To know there's still one of them here, that we haven't *quite* gotten rid of them and probably never will.'

'It is highly fortunate that our two peoples . . .' the Peke began, but Tito Cravelli cut him off.

'Save it. The campaign is over.'

'We're taking a rest,' Danville added. 'Highly deserved, too.'

The Peke blinked in surprise, then said hurriedly, 'As currently the sole surviving member of my race on this side of the . . .'

'I'm sorry,' Jim said, 'But Tito's right; we can't listen to any more. We've got to leave here. You're welcome to come along, but don't make any speeches. You understand? It's over. We've got other things on our minds, now.' The time you're talking about seems like a million years ago, he said to himself. It no longer seems plausible that your race and ours made contact during modern, historical times; the memory of it is beginning to fade. And your presence here among us has the quality of a startling and unexplained anomaly; it's more puzzling than anything else.

'Let's go,' Phil Danville said, getting his coat and Dorothy's from the hall closet and moving toward the door.

'I would think twice before going out there,' the Peke said to Jim Briskin. 'There's a man lying in wait for you.'

The Secret servicemen, again alert, strolled forward.

'Who is it?' Jim asked the Peke.

'I couldn't catch his name,' the Peke said.

'Better not go out there,' Tito said warningly.

'A well-wisher,' Jim said.

'An assassin, you mean,' Tito said.

Jim started to open the hall door, but one of the Secret servicemen stopped him. 'Let us check first.' They filed, hard-eyed, out of the room.

'They're still after you,' Tito said to Jim.

'I doubt that very much,' Jim said.

A moment later the Secret servicemen returned, leisurely. 'It's okay, Mr Briskin. You can talk to him.'

Opening the hall door, Jim looked out. It was not a well wisher and, as the Secret servicemen had said, it was not an assassin.

The man waiting for him was Bruno Mini.

Hand extended, Mini said, 'It certainly took me a long time to catch up with you, Mr Briskin. I've been trying all throughout the latter part of the campaign.'

'Indeed you have, Mr Mini,' Jim said.

Mini advanced toward Jim, smiling an intense, white-tooth smile. A small man, wearing a stylish but somewhat gaudy Ionian purple snakeskin jacket with illuminated kummerbund and curly-toed Brazilian pigbark slippers, Mini looked exactly what he was: a dealer in wholesale dried fruit. 'We've got a tremendous amount of vital business to transact,' Mini said earnestly. The gold toothpick projecting from between his molar teeth wobbled in a spasm of energetic activity. 'At this point I can reveal to you that the first planet I've planned on — and this will no doubt come to you as a complete surprise — is Uranus. You'll naturally ask why.'

'No,' Jim Briskin said. 'I won't ask why.' He felt resigned. Sooner or later Mini had to catch up with him. In fact, he was very slightly but perceptibly relieved that it had at last happened . . . and that did surprise him.

'Where can we go that we can talk at adequate length to do justice to this topic, and of course, in strict private?' Mini asked. He added, 'I've already gone to the trouble of informing the media that we would meet, tonight; it's my conviction, based on years of experience, that dignified but continual public exposure to our program will do much to put it over with the — how shall I phrase it? — less educated masses.' He rooted vigorously in his overstuffed briefcase.

A Secret serviceman appeared out of nowhere and took the briefcase from Mini.

Grumbling, Mini said, 'You fellows inspected it downstairs on the front sidewalk and then here just a minute ago. For heaven's sake.'

'Can't afford to take any chances.' Obviously the Secret servicemen viewed Bruno Mini with magnified distrust. Some quality about him aroused their professional interest. The briefcase was elaborately examined and then, reluctantly, passed back to Mini as being harmless.

From the room noisily trooped Tito Cravelli, Phil Danville, Dorothy Gill, the Peke Bill Smith, wearing his blue cloth cap and carrying his linguistics machine, and finally three Secret servicemen. 'We're on our way to Sal and Pat's,' Tito explained to Jim Briskin. 'You coming or not?'

'Not for a while,' Jim Briskin said, and knew that it would be a long time before he managed to get to this party or any other party.

'Let me describe the advantages of Uranus,' Mini said enthusiastically. And began handing Jim an overwhelming spectrum of documents from his briefcase as rapidly as possible.

It was going to be a difficult four years. He could see that. Four? More likely eight.

— The way things turned out, he was proved correct.